Visits to the Confabulatorium

Soramimi Hanarejima

MONTAG

First Montag Press E-Book and Paperback Original Edition October 2017

Montag Press
ISBN: 978-1-940233-40-6
Editor - Mara Hodges
Cover Illustrations and title/author font © Rose Wong
Interior book design and jacket © 2017 Niall Gray
Managing Director – Charlie Franco

A Montag Press Book
www.montagpress.com
Montag Press
1066 47th Ave. Unit #9
Oakland CA 94601 USA

Printed & Digitally Originated in the United States of America
10 9 8 7 6 5 4 3 2 1

Hanarejima's arsenal of emotions give the Confabulatorium an extra texture that is truly rare in literature these days. Nothing copycat here; no imitation; a defiant style that bucks the trend. This book has made me ecstatic for his emergence in a culture in dire need of such an authentic, fun, articulate and pretenseless voice.

— Zachary Amendt, author of *STAY*

Inventive stories from a new talent to watch. Some of the shortest stories here have the most impact. This is a collection with a distinctive voice, and Soramimi Hanarejima is a writer to add to your list. An impressive effort.

— Matthew Salesses, author of *The Hundred-Year Flood*

In this unique and charming debut, Hanarejima weaves vignettes of 'another world, intermingled with our own', where ideas come in standard sizes, and mental models are tangible... A visit to the confabulatorium is refreshing, rewarding - and recommended!

— Tasneem Zehra Husain, author of *Only The Longest Threads*

From the absence of curiosity in "Mismanagement of Restlessness" to the diagnosis of "lazy mind's eye" in "Anisotropy," the reality-unreality that exists in each story captures you, turns you around and then sets you down again, in the same place but different somehow. The stories in *Visits to the Confabulatorium* linger long after the last line is read, teasing you to return and travel along those lines again.

— Nancy Christie, author of *Traveling Left of Center and Other Stories*

Soramimi Hanarejima's *Visits to the Confabulatorium* is undeniably humorous and philosophical and exuberantly contemplative.

— Eleanor Levine, author of *Waitress at the Red Moon Pizzeria*

Contents

Self, Out of Focus

In the waiting room, I try to picture what my qualities are up to here, what I'd see if I had my glasses on: curiosity hovering in fascination by the painting of a space colony (probably on Triton) hanging above the vacant seats opposite me, impatience pacing about while reviewing to-do list tasks, making anxiety even more restless, love floating by a window, preoccupied by some romantic daydream.

Then I look at who is actually here: the rambunctious boy and girl shouting at each other, the woman who divides her attention between lightly chaperoning them and reading a magazine, the fully suited businessman thoughtfully crosswording away, the college student napping in the corner, head resting on the floral wallpaper. Despite their very obvious presence, there is an air of emptiness here with the invisibility of my qualities. There is a dearth of self, an abnormal absence of activity, an odd quietness.

As I lie reclined in the dental chair, trying to avoid awkward eye contact with the hygienist, I notice a postcard affixed to the ceiling, a little rectangle of arctic landscape. Now that I've spotted this scenic image upon the otherwise beige paneling, my curiosity must be up there wondering up a storm, handing her questions off to my imagination. Seeing the postcard with such open space around it, I feel like I'm now in a roomy alternate universe that is overwhelmingly rarefied and uncrowded.

I can't believe it's going to be like this for two weeks, until I get my replacement pair.

I sigh as much as is possible with the suction straw hissing away in my mouth.

"Everything okay?" the hygienist asks, turning off the motorized brush she's been pushing along my teeth.

"Oh, yesh, yesh," I murmur, mouth tight with dryness. "Juz tinking about shometing," I add.

"All right," she says, nodding a little before resuming work on my top right molars.

I close my eyes.

Faintly, I feel doubt graze my outstretched leg with his characteristic uneasing touch. He's probably wandering about, calling something here into question—the cleanliness of some part of the facility, perhaps. I wish I could say I don't mind his invisibility. I may be better off not knowing what he's up to most of the time. Admittedly, I take some comfort, however, in his ability to point out things that could be wrong, his knack for preventing trust from going all out. And while their scuffles can be everything from annoying to frazzling (like those times when they're all riled up and I have to labor to keep them apart, to sort out what's going on with each of them and between them), there's something vital about their tension and confrontations. Especially when each teams up with other qualities, doubt calling in his go-to, anxiety—trust partnering with hope.

The vibrations and pressure of the brush whirring upon my teeth provide some comfort in this episode of dentistry depopulated of my qualities. I delight in the idea that beautiful hands are at work in my mouth, separated from my lips and gums by mere fractions of a millimeter through latex gloves.

I sit at your kitchen table, sipping from the glass of cashew milk you've poured me. It's the first time your kitchen has felt this still. I think back to the last time I was here, when curiosity, while in

search of anything new and different, found empty instant ra-
men packaging on the counter and pointed this out to love, who
then prodded anxiety to prod me. That ended with me and my
diligence and creativity cooking everything in your fridge on the
verge of spoiling, leaving you with enough reheatable entrées to
last the rest of the week and into the next.

Nothing like that is going to happen today. The atmosphere
is inert, like a museum, a place where things are meant to be still
and observed. But a museum from which curiosity and inquisi-
tiveness and appreciation have been barred entry.

You dispel this stillness when you come back, striding in
with your spare pair of glasses, the old ones you have squirreled
away in the back of a messy desk drawer. You sit down next to me,
eyes locked on the glasses as you hold them in your right hand.

"Man, these bring back memories," you remark, marveling
at the now retro-looking design of the frames.

"Oh fwuzzles, yes," I reply. "I remember you wearing those
in Ms. Wynle's class."

Catapulted into remembrances, I shrink myself into what
was your characteristically uncertain posture during class.

I raise a tentative hand and say squeakily, "I'm not sure, but
I think the author might be trying to evoke some sense of sensuality in the reader."

Then I straighten up and deepen my voice to reenact Ms.
Wynle with, "Sensuality or sensuousness?"

"I... I... I don't know. Sensuous?" I squeak out, back to
hunching down.

"Oh yes, bring back the magic of early-adolescent awkwardness, *please*," you say, eyes rolling. "I *can't* get enough of it."

"That was *classic* of you. Always trying your hand at academic precociousness. Wearing it like a chic but oversized coat."

Grinning at our retrospectively comedic youth, you shove
your old glasses at me.

Taking them from you, I'm surprised by the heft they have relative to modern glasses, which feel downright airy in comparison. I let the texture of the pseudo-sueded imitation ivory imbue my fingertips. I haven't seen this stuff since freshman year of high school, when the material was rapidly falling out of favor with fashionistas and therefore the public. It's like your old glasses are a mini time capsule full of memories.

"Wow," I murmur. "Keep hanging on to these and in a few years you'll be able to wear them again when they're back in style," I tell you.

"Maybe I should just wear them now and be a trendsetter," you reply.

"I think you could pull that off. But be careful. Pulling that off might use up all of your cachet."

"All right, enough talk of fashion and the limits of my suaveness. Put those things on and see what you can see."

So I do, and immediately it's disorienting. We knew its prescription is different from mine, but we didn't know how different.

The proportions are all wrong. Confidence is huge, looming over everything. Hope is hazy, diffuse and nebulous, fogging up the kitchen. Ambition—I haven't seen him for a while—he's taking up the whole corner by the stove, lanky and angular. Anxiety is on the floor, flattened down to a mauve mound, like he has no will to rise against gravity's pull. The most normal-looking one is love, with her usual prismatic colors and slender tendrils.

It's comforting to see them, but their distorted forms will probably cause more harm than good. I can't tell what most of them are doing.

I take off the glasses and hand them back to you.

"No good?" you ask.

"It was worth a try," I tell you.

"Yes, nothing lost in giving it a go," you agree.

"Too bad I can't see your qualities directly," you remark. "Otherwise, I could describe them to you. But I can tell you that my sense of belonging is happy to have your sense of humor here."

"Oh, she's here, is she?"

"Can't you tell?"

"Now that you mention it, yes, I should have known."

"How did you break your glasses again?" you ask.

Did I not tell you this? You would have remembered this.

"A very friendly Samoyed licked them off my face."

You burst into laughter.

It's only a slight exaggeration. Some nuzzling and pawing were also involved. Gravity and pavement did the rest.

As I bicycle home, down the path lined with chicory and poke-weed, I marvel at how I completely missed my sense of humor's hand in our conversation today. She must have nudged me to make fun of who you used to be. Her touch has become so familiar that I don't even notice it anymore. I just notice where it ends up taking me.

What else have I been missing?

I divert some of my attention from bicycling, which isn't hard to do since I'm just taking my customary route and traffic is light.

I look at the leaves on the branches ahead of me above the path, at the way they glow with a bright, vital greenness as sunlight filters through them. I feel a quiet delight entering my mind. That must be from my sense of beauty.

Then thoughts of childhood walks with my parents and travels to Nolinga Canyon drift through my mind.

"Is that you, nostalgia?" I murmur.

I start pedaling faster.

"Don't worry," I assure anxiety. "I'm paying attention to the path."

I burst through the front door and cast my bicycle helmet to the floor, heading straight for the living room.

"All right, gather round," I tell my qualities.

I try to gauge their presence and attentiveness before I continue. I feel curiosity looking over my shoulder, wondering how this will go. Integrity and hope are urging me on. I can't be sure if they've all convened here, but intuition tells me we're all set.

"It's going to be two weeks until the new glasses are ready," I begin. "I won't be able to see you in the meantime. But just do your thing, and I'll try to feel out what you're doing. Or get my attention somehow. Give me ideas."

Then, there's a whisper in my mind.

You need to make time to feel us, our presence and activity.

"Insight?" I whisper back.

"You're right," I agree. "I'll schedule that into my calendar."

And once I do, I'm all ready for the next two weeks.

Consequences of Oversweetening

You are throwing my metaphysiology out of balance with very sweet compliments.

Throughout the workday, you commend me on everything from my project ideas and my technical know-how to my outfits, musical tastes and culinary suggestions, to my reliability, tactful honesty and listening skills. You've gone far beyond our culture of collegiality and habits of friendship, as if you're now forging your own code of relentlessly appreciative workplace camaraderie.

It feels great to receive each heartwarming nugget of affirmation, but the cumulative effects are problematic. Under the influence of your kind, appreciative words, I become prone to hyperactivity and hypercogitation; sporadically throughout my days and nights, I'm hit by bouts of restlessness, giddiness, jitteriness, wanderlust, fantasizing, pacing, trampolining, spontaneous mini-dancing, fidgeting and full-on insomnia. And the overexertion is taxing, just draining, both emotionally and physically on my typically calm constitution.

While this can be exhilarating and delightful, my body and thus career, even social life cannot function with the bursts of over-zealousness for life induced by the exuberant validation you furnish—*no*, lavish upon me. I have to find a way to mitigate the effects.

Fortunately, with the fervent pace at which my mind works while invigorated by your appreciation, I'm able to easily whip up a whirlwind of ideas. I find swirling in there a couple of promising possibilities.

1. Increase my metaphysiological metabolism through some demanding activity and expend the excess energy you've conferred upon me.
2. Devise a way to store your compliments, to postpone and thereby pace out their consumption.

The second seems more promising, posing minimal disruption to my daily modus operandi. I can just stash away your compliments when I receive them, relish them later instead of letting them rush right into my metaphysiology. Simple. No need to make any significant modifications to my behavior.

The next day at the office, I tuck into my memory each morsel of validation or praise or appreciation you give me. And throughout the day I am the most normal and the least hyperactive I've been in a while. In the evening, I have no trouble getting to sleep.

Waking up refreshed the next morning, I decide to treat myself to one of the compliments you gave me the day before. I pluck from my memory your kind words about my analysis of possibility density distributions and savor this comment along with my morning coffee. It's a wonderful combination to start the day with. A compliment and caffeine. Perks me right up.

Encouraged by this, I continue setting aside almost every compliment you confer upon me, saving them for later consideration. But soon I notice that by doing this, your mood is dampened. You don't see the joy that your compliments usually give me, and I see your puzzlement, then disappointment. I fear some unwanted toll on our relationship will be exacted if this goes on.

Abandoning this approach, I work on figuring out what the option I'm left with entails. Just what does one do when one must burn extra energy? There's jogging, but I can't always go out for a run. I need an activity or set of activities that could be done during work hours and other times of the day, like crossword puzzles or squats (neither of which I enjoy enough to do with the frequency necessary to ameliorate my situation).

I get to thinking that in most places, there are people, and most people are fine with good-humored chitchat. So I try drawing upon the origins of this extra energy: social interaction. Striking up conversations, throwing banter around, I let the abundance of energy flow into jovial words, jocular comments to friends and acquaintances, upbeat smalltalk with complete strangers.

But it takes an unexpected turn: I become flirty.

Fearful of acquiring a reputation I don't want, I try to come up with another means of expending the energy.

Soon, my jumpy mind lands upon the fanciful idea of keeping a clown costume in the drawer of my desk. Whenever I'm over-energized by your chipper, heartfelt words, I can get into character in the bathroom—conceal my identity beneath a puffy, polychromatic wig and thick, pasty makeup. Then I'll head off to the playground down the street, heartily greeting adults and children along the way. Maybe I'll take balloon sculpting classes to build out this new persona. A pleasant warmth fills me as I imagine boisterous scenarios of laughing toddlers and their smiling parents, of me waddling down the city blocks and telling jokes, of getting invited by grandparents to be the goofy, old-fashioned entertainment at birthday parties.

Before I know it, half an hour has gone by, and I'm feeling mellowed, even tired out. Then with a relaxed jubilance, I realize this is it. Not actually becoming a clown but daydreaming about it. Or about something else entirely. If I can't do an aerobic workout, daydreaming is the perfect outlet for the abundance of energy you're bestowing upon me. There are so many alternate lives I'd love to imagine out, live out in my mind, and now I can, one fantastical, quotidian, endearing or wistful episode at a time.

Painfully Perfect Models

"Honey," your mother begins, her customary term of endearment once again encumbered with concern.

And if there was any doubt about the seriousness of the conversation you've been called here to have, that bit of skepticism is now gone.

"These things are going to hurt you more than help you," your mother says in that characteristic way of hers that's so assertive and so loving.

Her gaze rests heavily upon the collection of mental models she has asked you to lay out on the kitchen table for this discussion. Then her eyes rise to meet yours.

"If you don't stop using them, we will have to take them away from you," she tells you.

You look to your father. Because although he is not more sympathetic to you than your mother, he acts upon feelings of sympathy more often.

Sitting beside your mother, your father seems reluctant to be part of this discussion.

Nodding slowly and thoughtfully, he says solemnly, "They're beautiful, but we've seen charming, exquisite things—especially ideas—cause people much distress."

"What about 'no pain, no gain'?" you rebut.

You want words that are more cogent, those that are fitting of the ideals you are defending, but the emotions filling your mind hinder your ability to articulate, leaving it easiest to deploy this abundant aphorism.

"You'll find out that at the other end of the spectrum is: 'constant pain, constant drain.' And that's what we're afraid will happen if this keeps up," your mother replies.

"Of course we're not saying that you should live your life trying to minimize pain, but not all pain brings gain," your father says, then after a moment of consideration adds, "Truly meaningful gain."

"Think about it, dear," your mother says, her way of concluding serious talks with you since you were seven.

"We'll talk about this again soon," she adds.

And your mind is left with no choice but to think—to mull and develop a plan that involves me, your usual accomplice.

You get up from your seat at the kitchen table and quickly gather up your mental models.

"I need you to hang on to these," you tell me, voice echoing slightly in the empty woodshop.

We're sitting on our usual worktable, you crosslegged, me with my legs dangling over the side. The tenuous sunlight of late afternoon perfuses the stillness of the woodshop meekly; it looks as if a wave of my hand would smear away the thin light, leaving a pocket of darkness. That in combination with the scent of pine creates a relaxed yet subtly clandestine atmosphere.

I expect you to give me some of those snacks your parents don't want you eating too much of. Or new issues of those magazines about designer furniture and home renovation and neopostmodern books and avant-garde films. But then my mind dizzies ecstatically as you hold towards me a set of mental models. Your ideals. Spectacular as always. Impeccable. Good thing we're sitting, or I'd need something to lean on.

For a moment, I have to marvel at the topmost one: the epic arc of humanity as a story of love on multiple scales. It's spellbinding. Astounding and endearing that you can think of the course of human history, of who we are collectively, in this way.

Then, with hands I can now only barely feel, I take the bundle of cognitive structures from you, then let them rest on my lap with my arms around them.

"My parents don't want me to use them anymore," you explain. "If they see—or find these around, they'll get upset. They think the expectations I form with them are too high."

"Too high is an understatement," I blurt, keenly aware of just how often these ideals involve lofty standards that aren't met.

"But you know I can't help thinking about how the world is already amazing and could be even better," you remind me, putting your whole body into these words.

But "better" to you translates to "much, much better" to the rest of us.

"I know. That's what makes you amazing. But also unhappy. Or leads us to make you unhappy," I tell you, again drawing attention to how I've repeatedly fallen short of your expectations, often inevitably. This might end up being another instance.

You sigh heavily and look at me with eyes seeking sympathy, eyes that reveal how precocious you are and how immature both of us still are.

"It's touching—it really is—that you think I sometimes am or could be or should be this prodigiously dependable, supportive, thoughtful person," I continue on. "And I try really hard to be that person for you. I would love to always be that person—my life would be so tremendously better as that person! But we all have our foibles and follies. We're all, to varying degrees, human."

"I know. Really, I do, and I am sorry about all that," you reply in a softer voice. "But once you see people, circumstances, places and all this stuff the way I do, you know you absolutely have to keep doing that. It has an importance I can't quite grasp, let alone articulate. There's some deep significance I'm not ready, not yet experienced or worldly or *whatever* enough to understand."

You look at me with incredibly intense eyes, as if you are seeing the way our world should be right in front of you, superimposed on what to you is varying degrees of imperfection. Although your mental models are resting upon my lap, your mind may very well be making and using new, similar ones now—as if donning upon you glasses that confer idealistic double vision juxtaposing the quotidianly mundane with the utopianly perfect. Perhaps you now see beside me or overlaid upon me a freshly constructed ideal of me. Someone who would readily empathize with this situation, know completely and unequivocally how you feel, what you're going through. But I am not this person.

I reach over and place my hand on your shoulder. I want to respond to your words with the affirmation you need, but instead of saying, *I know exactly what you mean, and you're absolutely right*, I can only tell you, "I know how much these mean to you. I'll keep them for you."

"Thanks," you answer, more at ease now.

We look past the lathe and bandsaw, stare out through the wide window, our gazes extending outward until they hit the trees and sky across the lake with all its waterfowl.

"Well, I'd better start making some new models that are more realistic," you tell me so quietly it feels like you've used telepathy, like you didn't jostle the air at all with your words. "So my parents won't worry. Or get suspicious."

Nodding, I smile just a little. Not only because you're more composed now that you have secured my cooperation, but also because I hope that as you make and use models that are more realistic, you will come to know their value. But I will be sad if you fully relinquish your over-idealized thoughts about the world. To glimpse a wondrous world through them is to potentially become encouragingly—*productively* discontented with ours.

I think about offering to help you make more reasonable mental models. But it's never been a question of capability.

The Captress' Co-Conspirator

When I set trap 77 by the solitary old willow tree now aglow with autumn morningness, 77 prompts me to once again reminisce over how we met, how we got here.

When I was in trap 77, as if held in place by the summer sunlight that weighed so hotly upon everything, my imagination clung fiercely to the bait you had set out. What I thought would be a minor delay, just a briefly distracting contemplation, became prelude to a lengthy episode of wonderment.

My imagination had homed in on, then seized that quietly wondrous nugget of still-raw idea, that combination of pastoral nostalgia and ecological awe which included a slight shimmering of the deeply verdant foliage coating the surrounding wooded hills, an understated vibrance evocative of the presence—even intrusion—of some greater reality. A subtle suggestion of proximity to the ethereal. It was so compelling that the new batches of ideas we now cook up for bait are still based off that old recipe you used for so long. Even if I had urged my imagination to relinquish that idea, my imagination would have held fast to it.

But of course, as was typical in those days, I exercised no restraint. And my imagination intently set to work on the idea, keeping me there beside a cluster of purple thistles in full, spiny bloom, making me apprentice to the examination and elaboration of the idea. From the speculations and memories I passed to my imagination, miniature mythologies were forged, strands of theory spun, then handed off to me to critique and revise. Then, together, we saw the landscape before us transfigured with this idea.

There is another world that intermingles with our own, a utopia that caresses our mundane reality. We glimpse it as subdued perfection, as sheer splendor hidden in pockets around us, transiently visible to us as the swaying of branches coruscated by autumnal sunbeams, the glow within particular smiles, a cool breeze off a lake on a balmy summer afternoon, the magnificently spread wings of a meerkat owl slick with silvery moonlight. We've misunderstood them. These impositions of fondness aren't surreptitious. Our ability to perceive them, these gestures of affection from one world to another, that way of seeing has atrophied.

We hadn't the slightest suspicion that this was part of a trap, an instrument to detain us in consideration, in an enthrallingly protracted moment of contemplation. 77, like all the traps you set, was so well embedded in the landscape as a mere tweaking of the portion of the world in which it sat, just rendering that region slightly more salient, intriguingly so. Unobtrusive and innocuous, 77 blended seamlessly into my perceptions of the dusty path into our town's suburban canyon. Totally concealed was the trap's extremely intentional and highly effective design to entice, to beguile and captivate. That remained hidden from view, until you came along and revealed it and its purpose.

I look over at you, across an expanse of dry, golden valley full of sunlight. Reduced by distance to the height of my thumb, you are setting the other half of the traps. I'll be over there soon, where you are, when we check each other's work. Then you'll just look at number 77 like all the rest I've set, considering only whether it is well hidden and properly rigged. You're not as sentimental. For you, our relationship is reminder enough of how we met. You don't attach personal memories to objects, especially not to the tools of your trade.

But to me, objects are sticky, easily gathering also questions about the future, retaining the wonderings crafted by my imagination. I can hear them now, as if trap 77 is asking me these questions that have been appended to it.

When you check on me later today or tomorrow, who will sit here, enmeshed within me? Or will I lie empty, the idea centered within me untouched? Or will someone's imagination have cleverly made off with that bait?

I know it's really my imagination beside me, like a ventriloquist, convincingly projecting these curiosities upon the trap. And together, my imagination and number 77 prod me to pose more questions, to engage in a dialogue of questions.

Are you ready to leap firmly into action, up to the task of holding captive a rambunctious imagination? Are you afraid you might end up like 49, mangled beyond repair and salvage by some ferocious imagination that can't stand any measure of confinement? Will you be as disappointed as I'll be if the bait is passed up by all the passersby?

The fictitious dialogue then attempts to become a triologue, with inquiries from me directed at you.

If later today we find a shrewd imagination here, will you or I make comments like those you made to me? Will you extend the same offer to the trap's occupants?

"Oh, nice," you said joyfully. "Aren't you quite a catch?"

You were smiling when I looked over at you. It was strange to have my attention shifted from all the thoughts my imagination and I had spun and woven in the trap. It felt odd to have my mind at last turned away from all the memories and images and stories and speculation entwined together. It was as if you had suddenly materialized from out of nowhere, though you must have been walking down the sun-blasted trail towards my imagination and I for at least several minutes.

You knelt down by the superbly camouflaged trap and dampened out the fascination field. Instantly then, it no longer held my imagination. Immediately my imagination then began wandering, searching for some salient tidbit of possibility to toy with. Looking at you, I began to see the trap's mechanisms of apprehension, very faintly at first as you reset the inner workings, just a glimmering where your hand was. Then it came to look like some geometric, crystalline object slightly displaced from our location in space and time, like it existed a mere fraction of an instant in the future and a mere fraction of a micron away from us in some ana and kata direction.

You stood back up, then said, "Good to know me and my traps, we've still got it," seemingly to no one in particular.

Alongside you, your imagination stood attentively, calmly ready. It made a strong impression on me with its confident poise.

"You do this for sport? Catch and release?" I asked.

"You could say that," you answered. "More like practice— keeps up my skills. It may yet be necessary to capture and harness the imaginations of future generations."

I nodded, finding a general truth to your words. Such a need could certainly arise.

You watched my imagination frolic and ferret out odd little musings here and there.

"I don't typically make this kind of offer, but I can help you train her," you said. "Maybe you think it's natural for her to run wild, but there's a lot she can't and won't do without discipline. There's some great potential in her that's going undeveloped."

I was touched but not surprised by what you said. During my childhood and into adolescence, I received various compliments on my imagination. Friends, teachers, relatives and coaches would enthusiastically mention the attributes they found admirable: flexibility, resourcefulness, versatility, eagerness and celerity. Their words gave me a particular pride which kept me from ever seriously considering anything even remotely resembling domestication.

So I wasn't sure how to answer you. I thought for so long about how to respond to your words that you decided to move the conversation along by going to your next point of interest.

"You overindulge her, don't you?"

Your voice was quiet yet firm.

"I do give my imagination a lot of time and stimulation, if that's what you mean," I replied.

"I'm not saying that's undeserved. She seems like she's served you well and done you a lot of good, I'm sure. But periods of moderation and temperance can modulate and sharpen your imagination's appetite, acuity and her intuition. In addition to keeping her fit and lean."

I became curious.

"How much training do you recommend?"

"Depends on what you and she would like to be able to do."

Beyond exploring possibilities—roaming fantastical and futuristic scenarios, intellectually treading along the cutting edge of our world—I wasn't sure what I wanted to be able to do with my imagination. So I turned to you for assistance.

And I asked, "What is it that the two of you like to be able to do?"

"Find and commune with thoughtful others and their imaginations. Make and share the ideas only we can together, those that allow us to be quintessentially human. There's more, but mainly, it's that."

And that caught my attention. Off in the distance, out in the star thistles, my imagination perked up and looked over at us. I had never explicitly thought about my imagination as making me more human.

If training would facilitate that, how could I say no?

Once I am sure 92 is set properly, having confirmed the nuance factor is tuned adequately for its location, I look at the sun as it hangs low over the distant cityscape. My imagination looks in the same direction and sees what my eyes do not. She then shows them to me as a montage of scenes.

I'm spreading cream cheese and plum jam on thick slices of rye bread, while you pour the coffee into our mugs. Afterwards, you're in the market bartering with the jargon watchers for their spottings of new linguistic nuggets. My imagination and I do reps of empathy exercises that make us ever hungrier for lunch. The secretboxes we've yet to craft all sit lined up in a row on the workshop table, each ready to keep safe the heavy, unnecessarily harbored knowledge that the future owners of these boxes need respite from. The beautiful lies which we will traffic for surprise and laughter, they glisten with benignly false promise.

I smile at these scenes, at the forecast they form. The day is just beginning.

Transactive Memory

We meet late in the day. At a time when there is very little lipstick left on your lips. At this point, much of it has been left on the rims of coffee mugs, corners of napkins and perhaps on the cheeks of a couple lucky people.

But here, no one else notices the dearth of rouge on your lips. As we stand outside the train station, everyone around us walks by like they all have some place to be, like they are each resolutely moving toward a particular destination in as direct a path as possible. They pay us only enough attention to determine how to make their ways efficiently past us, as if we were just inert objects in this urban landscape.

I, on the other hand, have attention to spare, and with it, I can observe you in expanded perspective, with greater context.

The fading sunlight allows me to catch glimpses of who you are not, your counterfactual selves faint and transient all around you. While you are distracted by the train map you're reading to plan out our route, I look at this entourage of people you could be—or perhaps more accurately, could have become.

The haircut you didn't get yesterday looks great. The plastic tortoiseshell glasses you never bought nicely complement the eyes of the counterfactual self standing by your left shoulder. Just behind her is a variant of you with drooping posture, wilted to the point of needing rainbows to prop her up. She is clearly frazzled. Maybe she was up reading late into the night, succumbing to that on-and-off habit you managed to completely abandon months ago. Her hair is like some domesticated animal in the midst of rediscovering its wild heritage, her eyes like they might at any moment close for desperately needed slumber.

To your right, one of these selves you aren't seems to be telling me something. She looks just like you, wearing the same crumpled, yellow linen shirt, but has no makeup on. She looks right at me, lips moving rapidly. I shake my head and point to my ears, not sure if she can even see me.

Then, as if she's understood my gestures, her voice becomes faintly audible.

"You will remember this the next time you're on the banks of the Shimantogawa," I hear her say as if from a distance through heavy snowfall.

"Remember what?" I ask.

But then she flickers away. Her place quickly taken by a nebulous alternate of you clad in what looks like a blue canvas jacket. I wonder briefly if you feel at all chilly.

"Did you ask me something?" you ask me.

As my attention focuses on you, these selves you could have become, they all blur away into invisibility.

"No, it was—never mind. I'll tell you later," I reply, not wanting to delay our commute to the recombinator by talking about this now.

"Did you figure out which line we should take first?" I ask, to keep us on track.

"Yes, Catapult to Jetsetter. Next train leaves in about six minutes."

"Let's head up to the platform then."

"Yup," you agree, this little verbal nudge of yours urging us along.

We enter the station, and I wonder what memory will spring to mind the next time I or one of my counterfactual selves visits the Shimantogawa. Will it be something about you or that counterfactual self of yours or something else entirely?

Mismanagement
of Restlessness

You get home, tired and relieved to be back. You're looking forward to having a beer and soaking in the tub, letting any residual thoughts of work evaporate away. But as you remove your shoes by the front door, your mood changes. Something feels off. The atmosphere is too quiet.

Shoes off and briefcase set aside, you walk into the living room, wondering if your qualities here at home are resting or if your hearing is unused to the stillness indoors after all the rush-hour noises you've been awash in. It sounded like everything was in motion out there.

In the bedroom, you find your qualities lying on the bed, snuggled in the lounge chair, and flopped out on the tatami mats. Imagination is just sprawled out in the middle of it all.

"Hey there," you greet them.

They wave languidly to you. *So they are resting*, you think. All the usual qualities are there, except curiosity. No wonder they're quiet. Without curiosity instigating play or exploration or contemplation, they're just taking it easy, especially since there's little energy to be drawn from you. Maybe she's resting too, on her own in a closet she's been rummaging about in. Or maybe she is here, curled up under the bed.

You head into the kitchen and get some ingredients together for dinner. Pearled barley, sweet potato, garlic, onion, curry powder, and spinach. When you open the fridge, that feeling that something's off—that vague unease—returns. Your curiosity doesn't come bounding in as she often does to look about the interior of the fridge. *Maybe she's having an off day*, you decide.

You start boiling some water on the stove and turn on the radio. It's time for that color therapy show, and that might bring out your curiosity. But as you clean and chop some of the ingredients you've collected, you end up listening to the entire show all alone. A little odd, you think, since the discussion just now on the benefits and applications of pastel purples seems like it would have piqued your curiosity.

Leaving the contents of the pot to simmer, you sink into the sofa cushions next to some of the qualities that accompany you to work—diligence, tenacity, integrity, emotional intelligence—all of you exhausted. You put your arm around your integrity; she got a real workout today with those clients. Kindness comes in, his presence warming the air.

Then, again, it feels oddly quiet.

Usually, she'll come find you, to bring you something she's found. You look over at the books and magazines you've left out for her, half expecting to see your curiosity there looking back at you. But all you see is the printed material left untouched.

And then you know something is wrong. Panicked questions flash through your mind. Is she sick? Injured? Did anything seem wrong with her when you last saw her? *When* did you last see her?

Anxiously, you search for her, calling out to her. You shuffle through the heap of undone laundry, open every cabinet door, pull out every possible drawer. But your curiosity is nowhere to be found.

With your analytical reasoning taking the lead, you try to sleuth out how she exited the apartment. No windows are open. The door was definitely locked when you got home. The veranda door is unlocked, but it's too heavy for her to open. Maybe she stowed away in your briefcase this morning or slipped out the front door when you left for work.

Then you realize that none of this will help you determine her whereabouts. However she got out, she could have gotten quite far by now.

You shut off the stove and dash out to check her favorite places.

In the sunset's fading glow, you comb the city gardens, hoping she might be exploring the plants and their arrangements or lingering by the oak trees and chicory patch she likes. She isn't. Then you walk briskly through the city observatory, along the path she usually takes to visit the views that most attract her. In your mind, you can see her perched at the edge of the path, gazing out at the districts that now make this metropolis home. But that's just an echo of the past or future reverberating in your thoughts. The path is empty, even of other pedestrians.

At the library, you go directly to the information desk and ask if anyone's noticed stray curiosity roaming around. The staff there tell you that no one has mentioned anything. They offer to get in touch with you if your curiosity shows up. You thank them and write down your contact information, then you head upstairs, to check her usual spots here, just in case. As you turn a concrete corner to enter the biophilic mezzanine, you think you see her by the far moss wall. Your heart leaps. Anxiously striding past little shrubs, you draw closer, only to find it's someone else's curiosity that uncannily resembles yours at certain angles, especially from a distance—the poise is strikingly similar, but the reach couldn't be more different. The remainder of your search in the library is considerably less eventful.

You skip the museums because they're closed, so even if she's in one of them, you won't be able to get to her. You'll call them tomorrow if you haven't found her by then.

Crisscrossing the city by foot and train and bus and taxi, you steadily run out of promising places to look, and disquietude expands to fill the space in your heart that hope is vacating.

And all too soon, you're staggering out of the city's only all-night bookstore, the last stop on your frantically composed search plan. It, like all the other places, is devoid of any trace of her. In a daze, you stare out into the vastness of the world while people pass by. It may as well be a bleak tundra or post-industrial wasteland of abandoned factories that's behind you. That's how dislocated you are starting to feel. Then guilt grips you, like it's descended from the sky and sunken its shadowy talons into you.

You've driven her to this. Kept her in an understimulating environment for too long. Neglected her and her needs. Made her ever restless. Certainly your intentions were good. You want to keep her away from all the mundanity of work, the monotony of the office, the banality of commuting and errands, the triteness of small talk. You've long intended to take her on evening outings to jazz clubs or weekend trips to the Nautical Hills, where the unicorn ranches are. You've been aware that this kind of dedicated attention has been overdue, but you were always either too tired or too busy on weekends, so recently you've been meaning to take an afternoon off to go wander the downtown neighborhoods with her, sample new foods, check out the architecture, and maybe try a crafting lesson. Or just go to that place with great tabouli and people watch.

And though she knows all this, her awareness of your intentions is not enough for her because it cannot fulfill her most basic of needs. You see now that the only choices you left her were to subsist off words and pictures or to run away into the world. The choice couldn't be clearer. She must have been yearning and yearning for something substantive to seize and tussle with, for fresh novelty to tinker with. So of course she would leave as soon as she got the chance.

Despondent, all you can optimistically think of now is that maybe she's still in the apartment building. Maybe she wandered into the basement storage areas or went into someone else's apartment and couldn't get back out. Slowly descending the sandstone steps outside the bookstore, you head back, preparing in your mind the script you will recite to neighbors to inquire about your curiosity.

What you hope will be your final train ride of the evening feels unbearably long. The seats, the passengers, the windows and floor, everything around you feels far away, your sense of perspective distorted, space amplified. Through all that distance, only the curiosities of other riders get your attention. Particularly the ones being engaged by children as together they notice things within and outside the train car. Then there's also curiosity being ignored by adults and sadly by some children too. *You don't know what you're missing*, you think. *Maybe because you aren't fully missing it. Yet.* The other qualities there, ambitions nagging exhausted middle-aged men and insecurities hovering around teenagers, you barely notice them.

When you enter your building, you see me sitting in one of the chairs in the lobby with my creativity beside me. You're surprised then glad that I'm here; I can help you ask the neighbors about your curiosity. I can take the even-numbered floors, while you take the odd ones. Heading over, you wave to me. Preoccupied, I don't see you, even though you are fully in my peripheral vision. You're about to call out to me and launch into an explanation of the situation. But as you get closer, you see why I haven't noticed you, see who has captivated me and my creativity. And relief overwhelms you, nearly crumples you to the cork flooring. *Of course*. You should have known. We have a lot to talk about.

The Company We Keep

It's just you and me right now, just the way you like it. In our usual, modestly patronized diner, we can enjoy a breakfast of yogurt,
figs, cheese, granola, bagels and almonds; can talk about your concerns without self judgement; can relax in this booth without Ms.
Timekeeper interrupting or Mr. Professional Development laying
a guilt trip on you or Mr. & Mrs. Idealistic-Perfectionism hanging some high standard over you to overshadow your accomplishments. They won't derail our discussions with trivialities falsely
made grandiose or urgent, won't dampen the atmosphere with
insistent complaints.

Because, without exception, my presence is enough to scare
off your selves.

When I'm around, the closest they'll get is hovering outside
the diner, peering in. Or they'll loiter on the library lawn, eager
to descend upon you when you exit, once they see me depart. Or
milling about the backyard, impatient to retake the house and
you, they'll glance at us through your kitchen windows. And
that's exactly where I want them to be. Out of our conversations,
but aware that we're having them.

I've made it clear that I can't stand them, that I detest
their criticism and overall negativity. I've also made it clear that
if they show up, I will make them miserable—argue against
every unreasonable assertion, defy as cogently as I can the sov-

ereignty they've claimed over your thoughts and actions, discompose them by shoving in their faces credible studies that contradict their attitudes.

Admittedly, most of them mean well, but too often, they get carried away. The manifestation of their caring is akin to overbearing parents scrutinizing every aspect of their child's life, and their concern for you can sometimes border on harassment and fearmongering. So you need a break from having this opinionated, vociferous entourage around you. And I'm only too happy to provide the distance you need from them.

But now, as you talk excitedly about colliding ideas (a pursuit the absent selves abhor as impractical), I get to thinking yet again that I can only hold your selves at bay for so long—this oasis we share, this respite, this lull in your intrapersonal storm, this can only last so long, until one of us has to finally leave for work or go run an errand or...

"But *of course* it's not just a matter of sheer force when launching ideas at each other," you say brightly. "There's the angle of attack, right? And here's the thing, even ricochet events can be highly productive if other ideas are placed in proximity, *strategically*."

Imagining you as an up and coming idea collisionista, I smile almost wholeheartedly.

But I am distracted by the fear that when your selves converge upon you after all this food and conversation, their efforts will be redoubled—the fear that this excitement of yours will be surrendered to and sundered by them. Then, there is also the nagging fear that they will conspire to prevent you from meeting me or devise a way to wear me down or to retaliate with their own scare tactics. I know what they're capable of. If it weren't for them, you wouldn't have gotten this stunningly far in your career, your relationships—your life.

But this is the fear that troubles me most: that one day I will tire of fending them off, that as much as I want to be around you,

I won't want to expend the energy, because I won't have enough or will need my energy for other things. I don't like to admit this, but I do occasionally think about how worthwhile it is to meet you like this; if it falls upon me to clear away your incessantly demanding selves *indefinitely*, I'm certain that I will eventually feel this arrangement isn't worthwhile. I am just uncertain of when that will happen—100 years or 100 days from now, those and many other durations seem equally probable. But I won't tell you any of this, because your selves would surely use it against you.

Instead of sharing my concerns with you, I've thought about doing one of these:

- Train you to rebuke your selves, especially when they come down harshly on you.
- Arrange a vacation getaway for you. Although your selves will surely tag along, their influence upon you will be diminished by your enthralled exploration of new sights and cultures. (In fact, one of them will be instrumental in subduing the rest; Ms. Maximizer will want you to get as much out of the vacation as possible and quash the protests of her companions.)
- Seek out your more supportive but more subdued selves, these aspects of you perhaps left sequestered in your memories or hidden in our encounters, peeking at us from around hallway corners or the back of the buses we ride, silently rooting you on. Once I've found them, I'll invite them to these breakfasts.

"So even if a non-head-on collision chips away only a prototype or salient feature, that fragment or the newly exposed surface can become reactive," you explain enthusiastically. "We don't need to go for integrative fusion or even massive fragmentation for recombination of ideas. Instead, we choose strategic launch orientations and confine the resulting fragments in a restricted interactional space. Or we surround them with inert ideas to prevent them from flying away after the impact, keep them within interactional proximity."

"Sounds like you're really on to something," I remark, delighted to see you so taken by your own thoughts. "You should try variations on what you've described and see what patterns emerge from the results."

"Right, right. *Exactly* what I was thinking. So can I borrow some of your ideas for this?"

"Sure, yeah, no problem," I gladly answer.

"Fabulous!"

Gleefully you press the huge chunk of cream cheese on the tip of your knife to the remaining half of your pumpernickel bagel, then merrily flatten the white mass speckled with bits of chive all over the toaster-crisped surface.

Now I know I *have to find* your other selves. You need to share this exuberance with them.

Seemingly lost in euphoric thought, you eagerly eat the rest of the bagel while I crunch through more granola.

When you're done with the bagel—and perhaps some of your contemplations of ideas crashing and smashing—I ask you, "Are there any particular ideas you'd like to borrow?"

"Surprise me with some of your new ones," you answer. "I know I've been meaning to check out your ideas in these get-to-gethers, but our time together never ends up being long enough to really get into that."

"Okay, nothing beats *blasting apart* my recent ideas as a way to get to know them," I jest.

You laugh—really laugh for the first time this morning. It lasts only a moment and makes me feel like I should try to be sillier around you.

"Who knows," you reply, leaning forward. "Maybe this is a form of intellectual intimacy that we'll come to desire more *and more strongly* over time," you kid in a voice hushed with faux secrecy.

Grinning, I shake my head slowly.

Then, coincidentally or through some unconscious sense of breakfasting camaraderie, we turn our attention to the figs, both of us plucking the little purple fruits one at a time from the little bowl of them. I have to have mine with cheese, the little slices of cheddar I ordered. You eat your figs after using each to scrape out some of the yogurt remaining in your cup.

Our rhythm of conversation alternating with quiet eating continues until the plates and bowls between us on the faux granite table are empty. At which point, we seem to be left with only a handful of things left to do: drink more coffee, pay the check, linger here as digestion runs its course.

"Well, I'm going to hit the bathroom," you tell me as I consider what the next five minutes here might be like—I'm leaning toward asking the waitress to refill my mug with hot coffee.

Seeing you get up and head to the back of the diner, witnessing that utterly ordinary set of actions triggers me to think once again that I should go with you, to make sure no self of yours pesters you in there. But I let this thought go, afraid that accompanying you would be overprotective, paranoid even.

My mind returns to the subject of your other selves, the encouraging ones I've only seldom seen.

"How am I going to get your positive selves to come out?" I think aloud, the verbalization making these thoughts more real.

"Oh, it's not so difficult," says a voice behind me.

For a split second, I think I've misheard part of a nearby conversation, but then my mind determines the voice is unmistakably familiar and directed at me.

I turn around and find one of my selves seated in the booth behind me, in the seat right behind mine. It's Qalixy, of course, with her torso turned so we're face to face, her arm lying atop the low wooden divider separating our booths. Across the table from her are "Dr." Relationship Manager and Ms. Brainstorm.

"Just be welcoming," Qalixy says. "Why else would we want to be around you?"

"What about my senses of humor and wonder?" I ask. "We enjoy sharing those attributes."

"Yes, there's all that, but that's *extra* as far as I'm concerned."

There's an intuitive sense that this makes. The trick will then be how to be selectively receptive to some selves while driving away the problematic others. Maybe that's not as difficult as it seems. I must be somewhat receptive here if these three have...

"Hey, have you been eavesdropping this entire time?" I ask them.

"No, no, we're just... hanging out. Enjoying the atmosphere," Qalixy answers as the others look on at the two of us. "It's so *welcoming*. Everything else is *extra*."

She smiles knowingly, and I immediately mirror her expression.

Anisotropy

After a thorough examination that includes various tests and interviews with specialists, my metaphysiologist diagnoses me with disillusionment stemming from lazy mind's eye: a tendency to shallowly, myopically focus on negatives.

She prescribes me a set of glasses to overcome this.

"They'll allow you to see beyond the little, troubling details," she tells me. "But wearing them is only temporary. After you get fully accustomed to seeing more holistically, you won't need the glasses. Your mind will know what to see and look for. But until that becomes natural, what you see with the glasses will be substantially different from what you see without them."

And sure enough, once I've got the glasses on, I see things around me—and ultimately the world—in a significantly new, better light. The dreariness of discouraging minutiae is no longer the dominant feature in my perceptions of the environments and situations I'm in. Petty annoyances and reminders of societal shortcomings shrink away to reveal the pervasively quintessential.

No longer do I see the litter around my usual bus stop as irritatingly uglifying this spot and my moments of waiting there. I see the bus stop as part of our massive transit system, relentlessly and reliably coordinated into effectiveness, an accomplishment then foundation of our economy, a vital circulatory system of our community, ensuring the steady movement of people, goods and progress. At work, the gruffness of my boss is superseded by his decision-making acumen and even seems necessary to the effective fulfillment of his numerous managerial duties. The nerve-gratingly gossip-ridden conversations of colleagues are subsumed into the intricate patterns of communication our species has woven over countless generations, a heritage of fluid, social information exchange, of storytelling, of joint intentionality—the glorious ability of two or more people to think about the same thing in a coordinated yet near effortless fashion.

This shift in perspective is overwhelming but mostly as a lush inundation of splendid, cerebral scenes, like I'm awash in some auteur's magnum opus—constituting its own genre complete unto itself—replete with gorgeous thematic arcs, intricately layered self-reference, epically prolific evolution, and mesmerizing profundity. And yes, some sinister motifs, but those are kept well in check by both pockets of righteousness and the broad sweep of unrelenting virtue.

Then, three days into this expanded perspective, I happen to see you in hindsight, as I turn my head and glimpse you behind me, tending one of the moss terrariums, little spritzing bottle in hand. The background of swaying, abundantly green branches through the extrapolatory's second-story window, this gently kinetic, verdant backdrop, adds the necessary context to see you more fully in and beyond this moment.

Gone from you are the unabating thriftiness, blunt nagging and propensity to rant about organizational dysfunction. All that is dwarfed away into an unmistakable, uncanny sense of responsibility emerging from sharp ecological reasoning and, alongside it, aspirations of effective leadership.

"Stay there for a moment," I tell you and also myself.

You give me a puzzled look but stay put.

I hold my twisted posture to hold you stunningly in my view. It's like I'm seeing you from years ahead in the future, when

I know who you'll become and how this self of yours now fits into some larger scope of self—that of a first-precocious, then-sagacious, integrationist visionary. As if with all the insight of an expert biographer, I can see how your greater self all emerged from what history has accrued to culminate into your character. Like I'm seeing you in some totality I might otherwise only glimpse when it is all too late, when we've drifted from each other, far enough for me to finally know that beneath all your frustrations is a deep concern for humanity—the legacy of your parents, the pride of your mentors.

Is this who you really are, I wonder. Who all the moments of your life coalesce into?

How much more of you will I naturally see once the glasses have transformed my vision? Will that make you more intimidating or more endearing? Probably both. But in what proportions?

Breakfast and Bias

At first, when I heard that she had toast in the morning, I thought it was cute. Who makes toast these days? It struck me as an adorably nostalgic anachronism, a leftover fragment of an idyllic era that never existed but that we had all been convinced had reigned for decades or should have or did in fact but in small pockets, like it had blotchily stained the fabric of society rather than suffused it.

Then I felt bad for her. The nutritional content of toast just cannot be enough to get her through the demands of a typical morning in the studio. Even three cinnamon-raisin slices smeared with jam would be ineffectual for accomplishing pre-lunchtime work.

And I began to attribute to the toast every lapse of proper grammar, each misremembered fact, all social awkwardness that I observed, assigned responsibility to the lack of nourishment the crackling cuts of bread embodied, pinned the blame on this mass without substance, on the absence of the better breakfast it serves as placeholder for or, worse yet, has ousted.

I considered giving her a bag of granola, a variety containing nuts and dried berries, but that felt too forward, inappropriately imposing upon her dietary habits. So I clipped out a coupon for granola and put it in my wallet in anticipation of an opportune moment to offer it to her.

But before such a fortuitous turn of events can facilitate the presentation of the coupon, I find out that toast is making a comeback, is the latest foodie fad among yuppie-wannabe hipsters, a breakfast practice that harkens back to those times that never were, should have been, or ran their mythic course in sparse enclaves. And now I'm torn between *(A)* concluding that she's been ahead of social trends and *(B)* surmising that she's an early adopter of them. Either way, the toast is in service of a status that she does not need but desires, like the toast itself. No one truly needs toast, unless the only available foodstuff is loaves of bread, and even then they could be eaten without the further addition of heat.

And desiring toast as one's sole breakfast item, that is immature and irresponsible. That I cannot condone. So reviled am I by this new information that I am driven to tear the coupon to shreds. But as it is held in hands impatient to pull in opposite directions, I consider that maybe it's her upbringing. Perhaps her parents left her with poor day-starting habits that went uncorrected all this time. Maybe she had a small dorm room all to herself during her college years, hitting the privacy jackpot while robbed of the chance to be influenced in a positive manner by a roommate. But even then, surely she must have come across a mention or two of the health benefits of a nutritious breakfast; surely someone must have mentioned how vitalizing scrambled eggs and fried potatoes at 7 a.m. can be; surely she—

"Think fast," you suddenly call out from behind me.

I turn around, and instantly my arms are flinging outward in your direction, attempting to intercept the binoculars now arcing through air between you and me. The optics hit my palms hard, and my fingers quickly curl around them.

"There's a marigold zephyr up there," you tell me, pointing into a patch of sky overhead.

Like some daytime meteor sans streaking tail slicing through the atmosphere, this swiftly gliding bird of prey catches my eye, and I raise the binoculars. Through the lenses, I marvel at its streamlined, gleaming form, its flight feathers indeed resembling the petals of its namesake.

Removing the binoculars from my eyes, I find you right in front of me, smiling.

"Thanks, that was quite a sight," I tell you.

"That bird always is," you answer, the smile brightening your words.

You reach your hand toward me. For a split second, I think you're seeking the return of your binoculars, but then I see the granola coupon held in the hand you're extending.

"I think you dropped this," you say to me.

"Oh, that. You can have it, if you want," is all I care to say, still miffed by my thoughts of her morning toast.

"Okay, nice. I think I know someone who could put this to good use."

You pocket the slip of paper. I nod, then look skyward, hoping to locate the zephyr again.

With the Clarity of Hindsight

At the edge of her favorite urban meadow, I rig up the curiosity trap carefully; I won't get another shot at this. Once my best bait is used up in this attempt, I'll have nothing that stands any chance of snagging her curiosity so thoroughly, so deeply as to hold her in the moment, keep her in the present as it becomes the past, so that I may see her in retrospect, perceive her with the clarity of hindsight. Nothing else I have will afford me the opportunity to know her once and for all, with that authenticity I've only glimpsed.

Once the trap is set, I get situated in the hide—the shell of a fruit vending machine, closed for the season. There, I put my patience into practice, to wait as calmly as I can for her curiosity to come along and be drawn to the bait by her intuition.

An hour goes by.

Then another.

Fortunately, the autumn scenery and my daydreams are mesmerizing enough to keep me lulled into a contented placitude. The occasional warbler and nuthatch that flit into view delight me.

Then you show up. You stride into the meadow, arms and legs moving swiftly like you have somewhere to be. I don't think much of this, simply assuming that you're just on your way to run an errand or meet someone, that you'll soon be gone. But then your curiosity leaps ahead of you, right at the trap. Clearly, it has discerned the presence of a promising idea in the landscape here.

I panic, rattled almost enough to jump out of the hide to stop your curiosity, but a couple of things prevent me: *(1)* raw shock at this turn of events, which locks me into the mode of being an onlooker; and *(2)* my left leg, which has fallen asleep. Immobile in the hide, I hope that your curiosity will simply examine then reject the bait.

But your curiosity takes hold of the intellectual morsel and plants itself right in the middle of the trap. You, of course, follow and walk right into the trap to join your curiosity. There, the two of you trigger the deployment of subtle, thought-provoking hints, and you become caught up in considering the compelling idea that stood the best chance of luring in her curiosity and ultimately entangling it, along with her, in a self-spun web of thoughts. Caringly positioned at the center of the trap now claimed by your curiosity, this recent fragment of wondering falls fully within your contemplation. Firmly, you apprehend it, this possibility of a maze so convoluted as to allow the meeting of one's self or selves. And it captivates you, draws your thoughts around it with its challenge to determine the topology necessary for such a maze, to design the structure required to achieve the encounter of one's own self.

I stare in disbelief at how ensnaggled you are by this idea, like this scene is an illusion that will vanish or come undone and yield its mechanisms of trickery. But there you are, defying my conception of you, intent on determining the quintessential geometry, the vital layout—how such a maze would have to fork, twist, and turn to present enough potential paths to separate subject from self, to de-cohere the two partners of personhood, then to allow them to encounter each other—necessary to show you, present you with your self.

Then the trap does to you exactly what I had engineered it to do to her. You become so engrossed that you recede into the past as I watch on, perceiving you more and more in your entirety, losing sight of the details so that I can see you in a holistic clarity. The themes of your thoughts and arcs of your life become visible.

And I see what invigorates yet troubles you: the deep synergy and contention between collective and personal progress, the desire to know what humanity and you are capable of, how far we and you can go—together at best, separately if necessary. You want the two to draw upon each other, for you to develop through humanity's continued ascension towards awesome awareness, for humanity to be elevated through your inherited duty to further its legacy. This is the relationship you so desire, an unrequited love that you've struggled with as you continue to better yourself while ever frustrated by the inability to directly connect your growth to the betterment of humanity. So much of what you do and who you are interlocks around that.

And that is why you are held so tightly in this moment of consideration that is now becoming part of the past. The maze you are mentally engineering is where you think you can find humanity, or some part of it, as completely—though only transiently—distinct from you. If only the maze were designed just right, in it, you could diverge then re-converge your aspirations for self and society.

I let the trap run its course, wait for you to complete the cognitive construction of your labyrinth, or part of it, wait for you to emerge from the other end of this moment, to rejoin the present, in possession of newly formed meaning.

Outsourcing Custodianship

This afternoon, at your kitchen table, you entrust your sense of self-worth to me.

"So no one can steal it or degrade it or otherwise mess with it," you explain.

I nod, then take a piece of pumpernickel bread from the plate between us. It feels as though the dark clouds outside have called upon us to convene here. But I know you and you alone have created this intersection in our lives.

I think you're asking me to do this so you can secretly feel psychologically indestructible around others.

"You can elevate and lower it as you see fit," you add. "I trust you."

I take a bite out of the thick slice I'm holding and chew slowly.

For a moment, I fantasize about hiking up a mountain and hiding it among the rocks, your confidence extreme and unassailable, until the elements or wild animals at that altitude take their toll on your sense of self-worth.

But of course I'm not going to do that. Physical elevation alone doesn't have such drastic impact on one's sense of self-worth.

"I'll find a safe place for it," I assure you.

And I do, but it takes me nearly two weeks.

During that time, as I consider various options, some troubling ones occur to me. I could

- place it at the bottom of my hamper and let dirty laundry pile up on it,
- tuck it under the sofa cushions, to be tightly sandwiched between them and the springs beneath whenever I or guests sit in the living room,
- wrap it in plastic bags and submerge it in the water tank behind the toilet bowl, or
- bury it in the potato patch and recover it during the harvest several months from now.

Surely few people would look for it in any of these places.

And you wouldn't feel a thing; psychologically, your sense of self-worth would be unaltered in these circumstances. Only I would have knowledge of the unsavory conditions it has been placed in, the location kept quietly to myself as a secret, terrible joke on you.

But, of course, I take none of these awful scenarios seriously as viable candidates. I do, however, take them seriously in terms of what they might mean about me. Are they evidence that I'm still upset about some history between us? Maybe the way things went in the entrepreneurship academy, where your venture got funded and mine didn't after you recruited away the talent I'd been courting. Or the time you tried to swallow your pride and couldn't hold it down, spewing it all over me in that fateful board meeting. Alternatively, is this the doing of some repressed jealousy, its way of prodding me from within the depths of my mind?

Whatever is behind this, it all lowers my sense of self-worth. What kind of person am I if I'm coming up with and entertaining such distasteful ways to treat your self-worth?

Days go by with only more troubling possibilities cropping up. The massive bag of kitty litter in the basement. The compost heap in the backyard.

Dreading the toll this might take on me, I consider confessing these thoughts—all of them—to Qalixy. She might be able to decipher them and tell me what to do, but she might also think less of me.

Then something odd happens. When the toilet water tank idea occurs to me again during breakfast at the end of a long week, I laugh at it, at the sheer absurdity of the scene I'm picturing in my mind: me lowering your plastic-wrapped sense of self-worth to rest on the ceramic bottom of the tank, the cold water chilling my hand and forearm as I crane over the open tank like I'm some eccentric artist turned deranged recluse in the midst of creating a scavenger hunt for myself. It's comical in a way I hadn't considered before.

For a long, dreamy pre-dawn moment, it's just me, my laughter and the bowl of oatmeal, all gathered at my little kitchen table. Locked in some serendipitous moment of epiphanal communion. Then the image is gone from my mind. I've essentially laughed it off. Just like that. Like I've shaken off anxiety or stomped away inebriation.

From there, it's easy to remedy my discomposure, and I can get down to the business of coming up with legitimate options.

Against the Misuse of Beauty

I watch as you pretty your self up, the first step in sending her out to lie to someone. She delights in this beautification you're deftly conducting, feels important with all the attention that you're giving her and the ability she will soon command more fully. Though she thoroughly enjoys it, I don't think you should be treating her this way.

After you've briefed her, after you've rehearsed all the inflections with her, once she's off on her way, I follow after her.

"Let's go see that new movie about the captress of imagination," I suggest as we're walking down the sidewalk.

"Sure," she agrees sweetly. "After I take care of this, I'll have plenty of time," she adds smugly.

I'm annoyed to the point of wanting to say nothing in response, but quickly and bluntly I reply, "You know what I mean," to move this semblance of a conversation forward.

Without slowing her pace, she turns to regard me with gleaming eyes, then returns her gaze to the stretch of street ahead of us, to the repeating pattern of compact houses and their little yards.

"Don't go," I say to her. "Is whatever this is about so important? Does it have to be handled with a lie?" I ask, wagering that she can't counter-argue this.

We are both well aware of the motif that has built up: her lies are seldom necessary, performed for personal gain she could forego, the exercise of a perk she has grown fond of.

She stops walking, prompting me to do the same, then asks me, "Well, what do you propose *instead*?"

She's forced my hand. I have to lay out the only compelling, competing option I've got lined up.

"I know it's been a while since you've gotten to enjoy the spa."

"True," she says in her considering tone of voice. "But you know what I've *never* gotten to do?"

Like a reed tilting in the wind, she leans toward me and whispers into my ear. There's no danger of anyone overhearing us in this suburban neighborhood. She does this for emphasis. But what she tells me needs no emphasis.

Her words widen my eyes. Then, done with her quiet, un-necessarily secretive explanation, she pulls away and grins at me. She really wants to know what lengths I'll go to to keep her honest and what lengths she can go to with me.

"Seriously?" I blurt, despite my certainty that she is completely serious.

She just looks at me with those darling eyes of hers. The sky behind her at once seems so bright and not bright enough.

She knows what she's doing.

My Lovely Nemesis

In the conference room I've reserved, you and I have our meeting to figure out how to proceed with our mutually antagonistic relationship. To determine new boundaries on heckling, to reconsider the extent to which third parties can be leveraged, to make sure the emergency contact info we have for each other is still correct, etc. As we talk these matters over fervently, I look intently at your adorable face which has almost always made even your snarkiest criticisms palatable.

Somehow, the discussion soon becomes entirely focused on whether we continue on with this relationship, whether it's worthwhile. We both raise compelling points for and against, keeping track of them on the conference room's whiteboard.

Pros: Builds character. Challenges our points of view. Strengthens resolve. Keeps us socially active. Prepares us to deal with other rivals. Maintains good posture.

Cons: Distracting/preoccupying. Requires a lot of energy. Emotionally draining. Spillover hazards—risk of affecting adversely people around us. Makes massages more necessary and less enjoyable.

When it seems like there's nothing more to list out and analyze, we both fall into quiet contemplation, still clutching our whiteboard markers, just in case.

"Maybe it's time we end this," you abruptly suggest, your tone very serious, untinged by any hint of your usual sarcasm.

My heart races, then limps along—I'm unexpectedly excited, then concerned, even scared.

"Maybe we've outgrown this dynamic between us," you add.

I want to ask, "Is there something else that both of us are growing into or could grow into, together?"

But I'm afraid.

Long After the Heist

The day after the solstice, I receive an anonymous phone call, from one of the women who made off with your intuition; who tampered with your therapist's coffee, exploiting his habit of leaving his office door unlocked; who then seized your intuition while your mind was open, your eyes closed, body supine on the couch, as your therapist conducted what you thought was the most freeform session yet.

I think that she has contacted me by mistake, that she's looking for someone else. But she tells me I'm exactly the right person. Because I'm "unconnected," I can now be involved in the return. She and her partner need someone to hand off the intuition to, to preserve their anonymity.

"How long have you had it?" I ask.

"Long enough," she answers, her voice still deep and low as if to command secrecy.

"For what?"

"For lessons to be learned."

"By whom?"

"Each of us involved."

"Okay, how is this hand-off going to work?" I ask, ready to proceed.

"At Conifer Park's hilltop fountain, you'll meet someone at ten p.m. tonight. Does ten p.m. work for you?"

"Yes. Yes, it does."

"Great. Maybe it'll be me there by the fountain. Maybe it'll be someone else who has been unconnected, like you. Whoever it is, this person will give it to you with an address for you to make the delivery to."

"All right," I agree. "Let's do this."

I follow her instructions, arriving at the fountain punctually. I don't want to blow this. Intuition is really important. You've probably been making decisions purely analytically all this time. That must be difficult.

I stand by the lit streams of water, which arc through the darkness like some vital energy through the void of space.

A woman sporting a bandana and generically hipster clothing approaches. Without a word, she hands me a parcel bound with twine, a piece of folded stationary tucked under the knot topping the parcel, as if it's the bow on a minimalist or low-budget gift, but this is precious beyond comprehension, indispensable for a lifetime of judgments—even if it lets you down now, it will refine itself over time; that is its nature.

The moment the parcel is firmly in my grasp, the woman nods and continues on past me.

I go home and open the folded sheet accompanying the wrapped item I presume to be your intuition. An address is written in all caps, probably so it's unambiguous. Beneath it lies a single cursive word with curious punctuation:

Thanks,

Like it's the beginning of a sentence that has not yet been fully thought out or that was intended to express emotions that, it turns out, cannot be articulated.

The next day I make the trip across the dense, bustling, leafy cityscape to the address given. It's a building on Mirage Hill, cast in an architectural style that once made it swanky. Everything in this part of town was gorgeously new 20 years ago. Now it's all a dated vision of the future.

Inside the building, I walk down a long glass hallway that hangs over ferns and manzanitas, each step I take as if upon crystallized air, until I find the door for unit 3A.

Upon this austere slab of wood before me, I knock with the knuckle of my index finger. After a moment, it slides open. And this is how I meet you.

The Basis of My Social Capital

Much to your annoyance, I've been granted a temporary monopoly on her discretionary cognition. But I, of course, am ecstatic to have received exclusive utilization of this nonessential mental resource. For the next several days, she will think heavily about my quandary of how to best allocate limited generosity, and she will become so intensely focused on it that she will likely come to the resolution that has for weeks now eluded me. She'll save me further weeks of frustration. Because she excels at this. In our circles of avant-garde intellectuals, she is known as the Crystallizer, the Solver, the Unstumper, Ms. Stumpbuster, the Epiphanist, an Insight Artist.

Her process is simple yet uncannily effective. All I had to do was furnish what I had in the way of information, speculation, and intuition: turn over to her all the progress, leads, and loose ends. All this she is now deconstructing to then reconfigure into the latticework of analytical comprehension, from which an insightfully explanatory narrative can be read out. All I need to do is check back in with her later this week.

"How did you secure such an immediately favorable response from her?" you demand. "I've been seeking substantial mindshare for weeks now."

If this café weren't so popular, you'd surely be kicking at the soles of my shoes softly and repeatedly, insistently.

You grab your cinnamon swirl off the little plate in front of you, and, like it's some sort of adult pacifier, you clamp your mouth around the pastry's crispy edge.

I'm reluctant to tell you that I just asked her, simply presented my case, and she gleefully accepted. I got the impression she was intrigued by the prospect of developing what could be called a Generosity Management Framework, like she could sense the insights my concerns might yield, the fruition to which they might be brought. It was as if this had transformed her into some business scholar enthused to create a curriculum for training elite recruits for a new corporate position: the Generosity Manager.

Before I can figure out how to tell you some or none of this, you lean heavily upon the table with your elbows, then tear the cinnamon swirl from your mouth. I look at the massive crater left in it, the irregular honeycomb of little air pockets now exposed in the depths of baked dough. As you chew intently, your face draws closer to my own.

A second after you've swallowed your mouthful of sugary and buttery carbs, you hissper, "Don't tell me—you're on the *A-list*."

Your voice is a precariously balanced mixture of resentment and awe. Grains of sugar stick to your lips, like they're the crystallized residue of endearing words or sweet compliments.

"What's that?" I ask, genuinely puzzled.

This is the first I've heard of her keeping any sort of list besides her task list.

"You don't *know*?"

I shake my head.

"You could be on this list without knowing it," you muse. "That must be it."

I infer that you're referring to some kind of VIP list. And my heart warms awkwardly at the possibility that I may hold greater social standing in her life than I realized—than you do.

But the moment is tinged with a sadness that puzzles me.

In the midst of folding my laundry, I pause, just as I'm rolling up my blue plaid shirt scarf. I let it sit limply in my hands, collar and cuffs dangling. The stillness of my body allows my thoughts to coalesce, as if movement would prevent them from settling into a coherent form.

And standing there by stout stacks of clean clothing on my bed, I realize that I don't want to be on the A-list. Or at least, I don't want that to be the determining factor in whether she takes on my conundrums. I'd rather my ideas than my personality hold sway over her. If my ideas intrigue her, that would mean that I have something to offer her besides my company, beyond my agreeableness to her views, to her hobbies and curiosities and communication style. It would make me more unique. The value I would have to her would be more deeply intrinsic to me, more deeply rooted in my intellect.

And this would mean that she's self-interested in my self-interest. That she has some selfish desire to see my selfish desires through, a yearning to see what I yearn to see decoded.

I want her self and mine to have such an intersection.

When I arrive, she's waiting for me at what has become our customary picnic table in the prairie.

We look warmly at one another as I sit down beside her, as if embracing each other with our gazes, that ethereal extension of our selves.

Does this only happen with people on the A-list, I wonder.

I almost expect to be enveloped in a magenta glow. Her eyes seem that bright. Her hair is unnecessarily, elegantly braided. Unnecessarily because her hair almost always looks good, as long as it has been brushed. On this humid, partly cloudy morning, she seems to be wearing yesterday afternoon's weather—snugly, like a tight sweater.

"All done," she says cheerily.

From her tone of voice and demeanor, I try to discern if it's my ideas or my presence here that delights her.

Should I ask her about the A-list? Do I have enough social standing—or are my ideas interesting enough—to merit a straight answer from her?

On the wooden planks of the tabletop, she places the system for budgeting generosity that she has come up with. Warped as it is by years of weather, the grain of the wood has an inescapable gracefulness—like it's the exquisite bundle of timelines rendered by a gifted chronographer—a perfectly grandiose background for what she has accomplished, the invention of her system a crucial event with impact that lies across several arcs of history.

Though it meticulously, astutely, and actionably makes sense of the quandaries that had so preoccupied me, her solution isn't at all what I expected. It seems to conform to a logic entirely different from the kind that reigns over my reasoning. There's no doubt in my mind that it's brilliant, but does it match what being human means to me?

Would the outcome have been different if it had been intended for you?

I hand her a jar of cashew butter ground just yesterday.

"Well, thank you," she says with a knowing grin.

Looking at her dimples, I wonder: In her newly devised system, is my gesture one of natural generosity, strategic generosity, token reciprocity, or obligation acknowledgement? Or is it just good, old-fashioned appreciation?

I hope she thinks it was a nice idea.

Learning to Live
Without Labeling

You can't stop using your new label maker. You're constantly affixing names and categorizations and terminology to everything around you, caught up in some crazed classification spree. Your dextrous, well-moisturized hands manically (yet still deftly) operate the little device that has turned you prolific in this genre of designation assignment. Though concerned, I don't say anything, hoping it's a phase that you'll outgrow—maybe it's just the novelty of the label maker running its course.

But when you label our relationship, summing up the connection between us in just two words that I don't agree with, this is when I know it's gone too far.

So I hire an ambiguity coach for you.

When I introduce her to you, you wrinkle your nose, then promptly label her and this intervention as "unnecessary" and "quackery."

Thankfully, she's not offended. Her eyes remain bright, and she responds with unfazed professionalism by considering your labels, then putting a label of her own over yours that reads, "unlabelable without further data." You can't really argue with that.

So she's able to get to work with you.

She doesn't confiscate the label maker like I thought she would. Instead, she has you do several habit-reengineering exercises.

First, she presents you with a series of blurry and abstract images that could be variously interpreted. You are allowed to partially act upon your compulsion, to make labels for the images, but you are not allowed to put any of these labels into use.

Then you move on to making several different labels (at least three) for each of a number of novel objects and situations she shows you. A woman paying out large chunks of attention for insight. A girl showing up out of nowhere and grabbing an old friend by the heartstrings, endearingly but disruptively. Some kind of plant that looks like vines of ivy but with dark purple butterfly wings in place of leaves. A book that opens to reveal that its pages are thin slices of toast, some of which have jam or peanut butter on them. And again, you are not allowed to attach to them any of the labels you've made.

In the final stage, you're shown ambiguous objects and scenes while the label maker lies just out of reach; it remains visibly present, but you're not allowed to use it or even handle it at all. You know you could use it and must be merely content with that capability—satisfied with the power you could but won't exercise.

After you make it through this training regimen, you go about your daily life under her supervision. When an urge to label flares up and you run with it, sometimes she'll stop you, grab your hand as you hastily reach out to a stick a label on something or someone; sometimes she'll swat away the label maker when you pull it out; sometimes she'll just crease her eyebrows; sometimes she'll simply observe, taking notes. In the evenings, you debrief with her in your living room, which has become your de facto conference room with her. There, she addresses your concerns and gives you feedback—praise, encouragement and criticism, in proportions reflective of how well the day went. Then she administers habit-strengthening exercises to overcome the lapses of the day.

This daily process repeats for a week and a half, at which point the iterations have culminated in successive labeling-free days.

In her clear, calm voice, she tells you then, "You've felt what ambiguity can be. Opportunity. The chance to see things in various ways, the knowledge that you could perhaps then choose a particular way of seeing and act upon it. But you don't have to. Or maybe you do. But you'll find out by embracing that opportunity, which you would entirely lose by grasping immediately for some measure of certainty."

You nod, while pervaded by the impulse to label what she has just said and the sum total of your interactions with her. Then, you allow yourself to be comfortable with the possibilities open before you.

Intimate Intimation

Early in the evening, I follow the arcane route of eclectic philosophical quandaries and science fictional scenarios aligned by your ambitions for humanity. Traversing that lofty, familiar path, I slip into your thoughts, the ones at the edge of your unconscious mind. There, my intrusion goes unnoticed, and to you, I am at most a vague inkling, a faint impression.

I get to work searching for any notions you have of the two of us being romantically intimate, ever eager to push one into your consciousness. Knowing they might be minuscule and nebulous, I look carefully, methodically. My treasure hunt is aided by the stability of this region of your mind; it's as if memories and biases and semantic knowledge here are petrified, utterly catatonic in comparison to the bustle of consciousness, that ever-shifting space of sensory experiences, impressions, analytical dissections, opinions, recalled memories, images, emotions and more. Now and then, a concept or fact is pulled from the environment around me, for use in your cognition. Nothing else distracts me from my task, and I move swiftly through the largely static mental realm of past moments and general knowledge locked into the lattice of long-term memory.

Then, after combing all your memories of our times together and scanning through your thoughts on them, after sifting through squirreled-away daydreams and lyrical whimsies, my systematic scouring yields nothing. Not even the tiniest, mundanely plausible hypothetical. My most promising candidates turn out to be duds, including the one I'm surest of: your memory of that moment my bare arm brushed yours on that afternoon in late June, an instant in which I was certain you felt some stirrings of vague, fleeting affection—a mere fraction of what I felt then. When I find this memory, I also find that for you, the moment was charged only with the tenderness of dearly held friendship.

My heart sinks with the weight of disappointment, the dismay that you've never thought about me with *even the slightest* romantic curiosity.

I'm about to leave your mind the fastest way I know how: to be expunged with the nuggets of gossip cast to the dismissive edge of your cognition, to be carried away with this social speculation that you don't care to keep in mind, that to you is wholly forgettable, is the riffraff of your thoughts that can only be destined for deportation. I'll ride the next rumor-jettisoning wave, this expulsion from your thoughts like the swift self-ostracism undertaken by a traveler ashamed to have committed a compromising faux pas, one that unequivocally reveals troublingly erroneous presumptions of the culture he has been a guest within.

But overcome with some exuberant desire, before I fully know what I am doing, I bare my psyche and jump into your attention, shoving aside your financial concerns and possible plans for dinner, pushing out vacation fantasies and fragments of conversations from work today.

For a moment I make you aware of the intimate facets of my self. Some of them you know well: those lanky artistic insecurities and disproportionately impractical aspirations, the robust curiosity and delightful culinary experimentation, that charming yet awkward sense of humor that reaches towards wittiness (while leaning away from snarkiness) juxtaposing with supple creative abilities. Others—like the banal fantasies of my middle-aged life abundant with pleasantly uneventful domesticity—must come as a surprise. The brazen exposure is total and honest, glorious and humble, sufficiently suggestive, compelling by virtue of the underlying universal humanity revealed, hopefully made more attractive by its specific manifestation in my being.

For you, this just seems like your imagination has gone wild, turned weirdly rogue. As if for no reason your mind's eye has turned away from everything it has just been looking upon and cast its gaze upon the idea of me utterly without superficialities and social conventions, in a sheer nakedness that inevitably implicates intimacy.

I stay in your attention only long enough to evoke considerations of our psyches entangling romantically. Then I turn to leave and pull at those thoughts, to take them with me into your subconscious and leave them there. But they cling to your consciousness with a tenacity that I should have expected, that is typical of your ideas. Now that I've come across your mind this way, you want to think about what it might mean, what potential it has.

I wait at the fringes of your mind, leaving ample space for these thoughts to elaborate. I linger there, in case there's a chance you'd like to bring me back to your attention.

Residue Displacement

The residue of that kiss clings to my lips, my palate, my mind, my heart. Now, days afterward, it's like my daydreaming self is kissing your past self. That gentle, firm pressure is constantly on my lips. When moistening them to practice the zonkoriaphone, I'll taste hints of the fresh wonder on your breath, that cool tang of creativity so very saccharine like an overripe peach, the hazy bitterness that imbues some of your words. That flavor, if you can call it that, is also faintly superimposed upon everything I eat, like extra, unwanted seasoning—a gustatory echo of you reverberating in my meals. My heart is tinged with your emotional identity—kindness, spontaneity, zeal for the sensual, ambivalence vying with desires—like a speckling of fingerprints impressed upon the tissue of my being. The thoughts murmuring in my consciousness as I felt the wet warmth of your mouth, that moment of mental monologue still faintly but unmistakably occupies the forefront of my mind. Like I'm still in that instant of interpreting the kiss as coming into contact with the ocean of your being, its waves washing over my being, hinting at a vastness that beckons. I think now that I'm still wading in that ocean.

It all compels me to wonder...

If you were to later kiss me again and later yet again, would different gustatory notes layer upon each other to form some complex oral symphony?

Will something like this happen after I kiss other people?

Am I unconsciously hanging on to that fleetingly intimate contact with you?

Do you retain traces of me from that kiss?

That last one I can speculate upon with some measure of confidence. The answer is probably no, because you act as if it never happened, act as if I should act that way too. You carry on as though the kiss is never on your mind and should never come across mine. Around you, it's like I'm in an alternate reality that does not contain that strange, heady moment. Like it could have just been a vivid, illusory dream. And if that's how we must treat it to remain firmly rooted in each other's lives, fine. The kiss can linger upon my lips and psyche but not in the space between us. The effects of the kiss can run their course on me but not on our relationship.

After a couple weeks of this, nothing changes except—crucially—that I want desperately to remove this persistent, vaporous reminder of you. I don't want to be constantly kissing a memory of you. I try tongue scrubs, cardiac cleansers, lip exfoliants, cognitive decongestants, and more, to no avail. The ultrasonic pulse massage, however, may have loosened the residue's hold on my palate. No longer reminiscent of a thin film of cashew butter on the roof of my mouth that obstinately endures after licking and swished gulps of milk. But that's only a marginal improvement. Everything else remains intact.

It seems that all I can do is wait for the inhabitants of time—diffusion, disintegration, dissolution, decay, entropy—to perform the chores of the universe that will eventually erode away these remnants. Slowly they'll vanquish the vestiges of the kiss, just as they have everything else that has ever seemed or attempted to be permanent.

Patience comes and goes. When I can't stand it, I seek a gustatory distractant, alleviate the quietly insistent vestige of you with artisanal lemon drops or a cup of pineapple yogurt, chilling and tropical on the tongue. Heavily scented berry lip balm is also effective.

The only upshot is that the glow ever on my lips keeps them a little warmer on the cold, foggy days of early spring.

Then I hear rumors that Qalixy has a crush on me, and while that's flattering, this development gets my attention for more selfish reasons. Maybe a kiss with her would displace the unremitting traces of yours, jostle them out of the present so they can fall into the past where they belong. This prospect gives me the mettle to make one of the strangest inquiries in my life.

"So, you like me, right?" I ask her when it's just me and her in the afternoon, standing in silvery sunlight.

We're back in the Monday room, to put us back in the frame of mind we were in yesterday while discussing Project Zanslad.

"Yes…"

Her answer is firm yet quizzical. Maybe she's perplexed that I'm seeking this confirmation.

"I mean, in a romantic sort of way," I clarify, just in case.

"Yes."

"Enough to kiss me?"

"Of course. Wouldn't it be weird if you liked someone but abhorred the idea of kissing them?"

Briefly, the thought of germophobes flits across my mind.

"But enough to kiss me for the wrong reasons?" I entreat, hoping that she'll say *no* and end my pursuit of this strange, long shot of a remedy.

"Like what? To make some ex jealous? To try some new kissing technique as a purely academic exercise?"

At this point, I have little choice but to explain my situation.

After I do, she thinks it over for a moment.

"Well, it is a weird reason, but I wouldn't say it's necessarily *wrong*," she concludes. "I would like to kiss you, and if the kiss has benefits, well, all right then."

I become excited but am still concerned.

"Do you want to think it over?" I ask. "Sleep on it maybe?"

"No—let's not overthink this. Look, liking you means I care about you, so if I can help you in some small way, I'd be glad to. Surely you've felt the same before."

"Yes, but this is some rather intimate help. And is it really 'small' to you?"

"Well, yes and no. It's kind of a big deal, actually. Emotionally. But it won't take much time and effort. Twenty seconds maybe, depending on how it goes. And what it really comes down to is also, do you want to kiss me too? Really."

I have to think about this. That last kiss was disastrous in its aftermath. And would kissing Qalixy get her hopes up or make things really awkward between us? Maybe right now she's fine with this... situation... this arrangement, but will she think poorly of it and me in retrospect? Misgivings about even having brought this up float around my mind. What a weird conversation for Qalixy to have with a person she's interested in. Maybe I should have brought this up later, once we'd gotten used to her crush running its course on our dynamic. I don't want to seem like I'm taking advantage of her feelings. It's all becoming complicated, perhaps unnecessarily.

But then if I just concentrate on the kiss itself, the moment of our lips and our tongues touching tenderly, then yes, I actually do want that on a visceral, emotional level, though I can't be sure why. I think it's because it would tell me something about her that I really want to know, that I won't know at all until it has been imparted to me.

Slowly and fluidly, she takes a step towards me. My heart jumps, then hammers. She's only a little closer but now fills my entire awareness. I look into her eyes. She smiles. Like she has authority over reality here. And proving it will be easy.

Then suddenly it's happening. Her lips are upon mine, our mouths opening to one another. My mind has to catch up to this moment, like it's been stuck on her smile, immobilized in that instant and must leap forward into this kiss that is unfolding now, that my senses and body are enmeshed in. The hot dewiness of Qalixy's mouth takes on immediacy and depth as my mind arrives at and then is pulled into the scene of this experience.

For long, fascinating seconds, her tongue caresses mine, taste buds grazing each other to offer a light massage. Tastes come and go in bright flashes of citrus, tingles of coconut and hints of cardamom hopefulness, enigmatic and compelling.

They first feel like the illuminated letters forming an invitation to her inner world of daydreams and desires, then they gain more form and force to become not invitation but insistence, a hot hand taking mine and tugging me toward a fantastical playground.

When it's over, when we finally separate, I need a moment to reorient myself, Qalixy seems to understand this and looks out the window.

I consider the... outcome. There is only a faint but stately sweetness, like hints of watermelon. Like Qalixy has deposited some of her voice on my tongue, left traces of a raw potential to speak words with dignity.

We both seem a lot younger and a little bit older.

"Well?" she then nudges me.

"I think it worked," I murmur with a grin coming on.

"Good," Qalixy says firmly.

She squeezes my upper arm lightly with her hand. With a gait full of self-assurance, she strides out into the hallway.

In the evening, I marvel at my newly regained oral normalcy. I'm able to enjoy dinner with all the zing of garlic and cilantro and pink peppercorn in my zucchini macaroni and cheese uncomplicated by echoes of you reverberating on my palate. Dinner is finally just *dinner*.

At last, I am no longer gustatorily preoccupied by you, by that intimate moment you don't acknowledge in the slightest, not even with a hint of awkwardness.

My heart is no longer permeated by your essence but is now suffused with a glad puzzlement, this warm perplexity supplanting even your kindness.

When I see Qalixy the next day, all I can do is smile, and in the smiles she returns is a clear understanding of my appreciation. During the day, we don't talk, both needing time to let yesterday's strangely utilitarian expression of affection continue running its course, to more fully unfurl in our psyches.

But two days later, the aftereffects of your kiss creep back into my mouth and stake their claim upon my heart once again. I notice it in the morning, right after I wake up, faint but unmistakable. As if I've dreamt about that episode of oral contact between us, then carried its vestiges into reality.

While toasting my crumpets for breakfast, I entertain hopes that it's just some sort of flashback, just the memory of those tastes resurfacing in a sensory manner. Maybe I'm conjuring it up, the way looking at lemons produces that phantasmal sour taste.

Hours later, to my dismay, it only becomes more pronounced. When the morning seminar convenes at 10 a.m., I first go straight for the coffee served outside the conference room, because that peachy sweetness is back in full force. As the seminar speaker is describing the efficacy of different people-watching hides (ranging from cheap laptops and newspapers to colleagues posing as friends in conversation and towers of Jenga blocks), I notice my lips are increasingly tinged with hints of warmth, long after my cup of coffee has been fully consumed. And traces of your kindness are working their way back into my heart.

By the middle of the afternoon, it's like Qalixy and I had never kissed.

Consternation quickly transmutes into the suspicion that this condition is self-generating. It continues creating itself. Qalixy's kiss nearly obliterated it, but the remnants have amplified themselves, restoring their former grandeur.

"Is that so?" Qalixy muses after I confess to her this reassertion of the previous oral state of affairs.

For a very quiet, motionless minute or so, we just stand there, in the coffee room that always smells like a recently cleaned refrigerator. The more eventless seconds sprawl out before us, the more conscious I become that I'm half expecting her disappointment to become palpable at any moment, thicken the air like emotional humidity, gentle yet uncomfortable warmth. This awareness is surprising because Qalixy has always struck me as the kind of person who, despite her competitive nature, does not deal in disappointment, opting instead for acceptance followed by action.

Stirring this scene in the coffee room back to life, she leans towards me, and I wonder if she's heading in for a more aggressive, longer kiss, one that will utterly ravage the reconstruction of yours, quite possibly with collateral damage.

But her head moves toward my right shoulder, and she stops when our cheeks are a few inches apart.

"I know what will work, at least for a *good* while," she assures me in a whispered voice. "But we can't do it here."

Her certainty is alluring. Then I start to worry about how much the stakes have risen now.

She pulls away and looks very deeply into my eyes. A promise is made between our psyches. I need a moment to understand it, but there is no question that I am going to abide by it.

Appropriate Appropriation

I've tumbled headlong into a romantic relationship with your doppelgänger. This is, in part, the outcome of the long-standing crush I've had on you, as if it saw in her its last chance at consummation.

She's just like you, but with some quirky differences and more sarcastic spunk, which really works for her and I think for me too. Basically, it's like I'm now in a love affair with a parallel universe counterpart of you.

Now and then, I wonder if I should tell her about you. Maybe she already knows who you are—I may have mentioned you to her in passing. Maybe she's even met you, your paths crossing as those of doppelgängers sometimes do. But it's unlikely that she knows about my romantic feelings for you, the origins of my attachment to her. I've kept my attraction to you well hidden within my psyche—aside from occasionally flirting with you, but that's all in the past and went nowhere.

These emotions don't seem important, but perhaps for honesty's sake I should reveal them to her. But why introduce this wildcard into our relationship? It might conjure in her mind a storm of all the unproductive but still troubling philosophical questions about love.

*Do you really love me for **me**?*
In your eyes, what's unique in me that makes me better than everyone else?

Would you—or really any of us—fall in love with someone who's just close enough to our preferences?
Is it really about me or some ideal that I resemble?
What if I lost my sense of humor or became invisible—would you still love me?

I've long since answered such questions, and I could honestly share my answers with her, but getting authentically philosophical about romantic love at this stage of a relationship is seldom helpful, regardless of the involvement of doppelgängers. My views on the nature of romance might just inject doubt into the still-settling foundation of our couplehood.

For weeks I try to come to a decision about how transparent to be, leaning ever toward not dishonesty exactly but secrecy, *selectivity*. Until the decision about what to do with these emotions is made for me.

"Oh, how just *darling* of you," she says suddenly, voice glistening with an odd delight.

I have no idea what she's talking about. My head jerks up, and I look around and find her beaming face. She's now to my left, sitting cross-legged, and nearly all our picnic paraphernalia is packed up. I must have dozed off, sedated by all the carbs we've feasted upon out here.

Her gorgeous eyes are fixed upon something she's holding. My gaze follows hers downward. Then I see my feelings for you in her hands. All of them.

"I always suspected you felt this way, but you're even more enamored than I thought," she says with glee.

Her voice lacks any edgy sarcasm, and I get very nervous. This must be some bizarre calm before the storm. I look at her almost maniacal smile, dreading. She turns her head to face me. My eyes focus past her upon the grassy hills behind her, as if unwilling to see the situation I'm now in, like a kind of sensory denial.

"You've been holding out on me all this time," she continues. I'm blushing heavily now, and soon I'll be damp with sweat.

"Yes," I murmur, making the weakest admission of my life.

"How could you?"

I'm speechless, just too flabbergasted, too ashamed to explain myself.

"If you *adore* me this much, with so much more ardency, why didn't you just tell me or *show* me? Why did you hold back?"

"Well, you know, I... didn't want to come on too strong," I somehow answer in the seconds before I'm hit by the realization that this is going in a very different direction than I had thought.

"You know how everyone says that scares people off," I add, finding it all too easy to head down the path she has put us on.

And having managed to come up with something plausible, I get caught up in the momentum of it and continue on.

"I didn't want to be seen as infatuated or clingy or overzealous. I didn't want to freak you out."

"Oh, you're so right about that last part. I would freak out. I *am* freaking out. What a treasure trove!"

"Well, I'm glad you're okay with them," is all I can say.

"*Okay* is an understatement. These are just *stunning*. I'm just bowled over by all these unexpected emotions."

I smile, not with vicarious joy but with the relief that we're not mired in some emotional disaster right now.

"I can have these, right? I mean now. Right this very moment. I just can't wait now that I know all about them," she says.

"Yes, yes, of course," I reply. "I was hoping they'd be a nice surprise, someday when you wouldn't be, um, well, upset by them. Turns out that someday is today!"

She kisses me on the cheek.

"I really must get to Trindy's tea time," she says, rising to her feet. "And this will surely be *quite* the topic to talk about!"

As she bounds off, hugging the bundle of affections to her chest, I grow ever uneasier. Is there anything in those affections that will give everything away? Is there some fondness for an attribute that you have that she doesn't that will expose the truth? Maybe I can get ahold of these emotions while she's asleep or out somewhere and remove anything incriminating. But then, with those beginnings of a plan, I wonder if I will ever see those feelings or her again.

My physical strength goes from me, and gravity pulls at my torso until my back is pressed to the now-barren picnic blanket. I stare up into the vast blue ocean of air.

Was she just acting? Did she know the true nature of those feelings and simply pretend that they were for her? Was she waiting for me to confess so she could stop acting and forgive me, making me forever grateful for her magnanimity? Or would she have continued acting innocent as I apologized and explained and apologized further? Did I just fail the romantic test of a lifetime? Or is this her way of resolving or removing this issue or obstacle or whatever it was in our relationship?

Whatever the case, I have absolutely no romantic feelings for you now.

Long After the Departure

As you look at the sculpture of career quandaries—at ambivalence given substance, apprehensions made palpable in unruly metal and marble—the nature of the struggle depicted reminds me that you would see this all very differently if he were here. But he now exerts no sway over your perceptions, over your thoughts and emotions, except only weakly through memories.

I still don't know in what proportions that's tragic and fortuitous, even years after the end of his era of influence over your life.

I stare up through all the humidity into the cloudless summer sky and revisit the past, its nature more dream than memory now.

Abruptly, he was gone. It was a Wednesday. He wandered off or you lost track of him. I'm not clear on what happened, but what happened next has always been clear to me. Once you lost your ambition, you didn't miss him, you didn't go look for him. You just carried on without him. Tired of his provocations, sick of his demands, you were ready to let him go—you had in fact been ready for a long time without fully knowing it.

If he wanted to come back, he could. That was your attitude. He could find his way back if he wanted to, and you wouldn't turn him away if he did return. The way you saw it, he needed you more than you needed him. What could he possibly be without you to pay attention to him, to do his bidding? You, on the other hand, would be fine without him. And you were. In fact, you immediately felt better off without him: less stressed, less uptight, less aggressive, still focused but not ferociously, not at the cost of reflection and relationships. And that has persisted, forming a lifestyle and an identity you've become enchanted with.

And I like you better this way—as do many people—but is this truly better for you?

Every time this uncertainty hits me, it takes me a while to figure it out, to remember what it's actually about. My ambivalence is really the manifestation of guilt. I should have looked for him with you. Or at least should have encouraged you to look rather than shrug off the situation. I should have prodded you to consider reconciliation. Instead, I played some role—a passive one but a role nonetheless—in letting what could have been a temporary separation unspool into permanent estrangement. I was quietly, secretly happy to have him disappear. It was always difficult for him and me to get along. And I was ecstatic at the promise of getting some of the vast attention you devoted to him. But am I the rightful recipient of that attention? Would you be better off in a rocky relationship with ambition?

Ambition could have taken you much further than I ever can in particular directions, maybe in the directions that matter most. You'd have more influence, stature, and probably wealth.

But he can never show you what I have.

You remain mesmerized by the molded materials before us, by the frozen scene of choices and their impending, sprawling consequences—webs of benefits and drawbacks—pulling at the psyche, each wanting to lead the psyche into its future. But their persistent tugging and their fierce competition is only possible because the psyche clings to them, has not let any go. The intricate contours of the rendering make this apparent but not obvious. The outcome is not a question of which pulls hardest but of which are released and which is retained.

So richly invested now with meaning by you and me, the artwork before us feels inescapable and inevitable, like the sum total of history must for us now culminate here. But we know that there is truer reality of sheer incidentality; this is just one of myriad experiences interpretable as discovery within the wending journey we've embarked upon without him.

Second Person Voice

I begin to suspect that you are using my voice to placate your self, maybe by telling her lies. I hate to think this of you, but you've lied to your self before, and lately, she's been unusually content. Which is especially peculiar considering that little has changed in your life, which she has vehemently urged you to reshape. So I have to wonder if you're using my voice to calm your self down, to say to her the reassuring phrases I've said to her when she's distraught. I have to wonder if you've contorted these phrases to be effective in a different context, to tame her aspirations for a future better than the one you're coasting into.

These concerns nag at me—worrying me in the shower, preoccupying me as I eat my meals, troubling me during my commute—weighing upon me to the point where they need to be confirmed or dispelled. I am driven into cycle after cycle of contriving, then reworking, then scrapping plans to eavesdrop on your private conversations with your self.

Until I'm standing in line for pecan rolls at the Nihuhu Bakery and a feasible approach bursts into my consciousness with utter clarity. I'll ask for my voice back to see if it readily articulates phrases you might be lulling your self with. This will take some trial and error, but I have promising starting points from which to explore the muscle memory you may have built up in my voice. I'll begin speaking the phrases I've said to her during difficult times and see if from there my voice forms the words you've spoken to her, jumps to the phrases most recently and frequently said. It should only take an hour or two of verbal exploration, of running through the beginnings of certain sentences.

As work is drawing uneventfully to a close on this Wednesday afternoon, I write you a short note telling you that I need my voice to catch up with an old friend who is in town. An hour later I'm at your place, standing in front of you, handing you this brief message. You nod, then withdraw my voice from your pocket, where you normally keep it when you're not using it.

"Thanks, I'll get it back to you soon," I tell you, finding it strange to be talking with and hearing my voice again.

"No, no, *no*. Thank *you*, and whenever you could let me, I'd love to borrow it again," you reply. "I'm still surprised by how little you need it."

"Well, you know how I prefer not to talk, and the telepathy technology I've been piloting for work has been *terrific*. Really cuts down on misunderstandings in meetings. And telepathy is *fast*. Too fast sometimes."

"Nice," you reply, nodding thoughtfully.

Then, as if jointly, collaboratively delirious, we're both smiling widely. Because I'm ever delighted by the telepathic technology and humored by the awkward moments it can lead to. And because you're imagining an extreme version of those kinds of embarrassing incidents.

"Care to come in for a drink or a sandwich?" you offer. "We'd be happy to have you over for a little while."

"Thanks, but I should cook some zucchini that's getting old and do some telepathic journal entries for work."

"All right. Don't get too comfortable living in the future," you tell me.

As I ride the train home, I gaze at the warm glow of the pre-sunset sky. It feels like some grandiose preview to a magnificent revelation. But, anticlimactically, I arrive home as I always do, and my neighborhood is as quaint and quiet as ever.

After dinner, I make some hot ginger water with lemon and honey to relax my voice. As I sit in my lounge chair, I sip the steaming, soothing liquid from a mug. I begin with familiar words.

"It's all right to just *be* for a little while."

I pause, hoping I'll be pulled or at least nudged in a particular direction. But there's not even the faintest inkling of a possible direction. I try again.

"Savor the present moment, who you are now with all your kindness and curiosity."

I wait. Then, when nothing comes, I continue.

"Embrace those qualities first and move forward in full possession of your positive attributes."

Silence again. I move on to something else I've said before.

"Without you there is no me."

Effortlessly these lead me right to more of their ilk.

"We emerge from each other."

But quickly, those lead to unfamiliar words.

"We first met, tentative and uncertain, that overcast day in early spring. You appeared out of nowhere and clung to me shakily, as if I could help you find your footing."

I clamp a hand over my mouth.

It's my voice telling your story, the story you tell your self. And though I'd love to hear it, I should hear it from you, with your voice, the version you want to share. Now I know why you've kept my voice for so long. You've been putting it to substantial and admirable use.

Nature via Nurture vs. Nature

This time, you're leaning just slightly over the kitchen counter, encroaching upon it just enough so the eye drops you blink out with the flutter of your eyelids plunge quietly into my mug of coffee. You don't notice. Neither do I. I'm at the stove, pan-toasting our bagels, making sure they acquire the crisp and dense consistency that only the application of heat through cast iron seems capable of conferring.

When we sit down to breakfast, we are utterly unaware that my morning meal contains an extra ingredient. My now imperceptibly salted coffee contains the residue of scenes you saw during the week. I gulp down those remnants as we crunch through our bagels, each mentioning our morning musings now and then.

"We're out of sleep clarifier," you tell me. "Can you pick some up? I'll be working a little late today and won't have a chance to get any."

"Sure. I can easily get that on the way home," I answer.

"Thanks," you reply, attention then turned to the tree outside the window.

Nuthatches cling to the trunk, their beaks angling out into this bright summer morning. Their posture looks awkward from my human perspective, like a person leaning out a window with head obliquely thrown back for a look around.

From the serene look on your face, they must appear graceful to you.

In the hours that follow, gratuitous acts of generosity flash by my mind's eye. They seem to come out of nowhere at random times. As the train slows to a stop at my usual station, in my thoughts appears a man foisting shades of green on a chromatically impoverished kid until she's smothered in chartreuse. In the middle of my team's morning meeting, I space out into what feels like a short, vivid daydream in which generosity drives a tween to unnecessarily "help" a senior citizen (who isn't even having any perceptible difficulty) cross the street; this apparently clueless youngster offers unwanted assistance to the point of hindrance and certainly annoyance, which the grey-haired gentleman seems too polite to express. While waiting in the lunch line, I'm considering the intern's project feedback when those thoughts are abruptly shoved aside by the frenetic episode of a hip urbanite giving a tourist suggestion after suggestion. In the thrall of his generosity, he runs through his top picks in all the city-life categories that occur to him: fine dining, museum-going, nightlife, bakeries, parks. Included with most are directions and recommendations: don't take bus 45 to the wharf, take the yellow-line train instead; get the scones at Bernie's Baking Bonanza; the glassblowing studio becomes crowded after 3 p.m. The newcomer to this city tries to politely excuse herself and begins to walk down the street, only to have the overenthusiastic denizen follow after her, saying, "Oh, *oh*, just one more place you *have to go*." This mental scene, like the over-enthused city dweller, won't let go. Chantrall has to nudge me to move down to the entree station, to close the now 4-foot gap between me and the guy ahead of me. Which I do, zombie-like, still distracted by the ever-persistent urbanite.

The afternoon, thankfully, is uninterrupted by this unusual mental imagery. Until the colloquium.

While I'm sitting beside my team members in the auditorium, listening to methods for becoming productively bored, my mind is pounded by an unrelenting rhythmic surf of successive images of generosity being forcibly restrained, denied opportunities to intervene and express itself. While standing beside a barrel stuffed with umbrellas, a woman watches people walk by, all of them getting drenched by huge drops of hard rain. In an open-plan office, a man watches his colleagues working frantically on an approaching deadline. As twenty-somethings with aspirations of founding startups deliver elevator pitches to a coaching panel of seasoned entrepreneurs, one panelist is keenly aware of just how amateur all the value propositions and personas are. But she says nothing.

Each of these onlookers has had his or her generosity meticulously and securely bound and gagged.

I'm completely baffled by these... daydreams? Is that what they are? Until now, I've never seen anything like this—generosity made to look on impotently at need. Nothing even remotely resembling them has shown up in my life, in films I've watched, or in my imagination. During a lull in the bizarre mental montage, questions pop into my mind, one after another, filling in the vacuum left by those scenes, filling the cognitive space now open after the images have shoved away all my thoughts. Why would anyone inhibit generosity in these ways? Why would my mind be coming up with these things? Are these repressed memories, suddenly resurfacing? Am I the unknowing subject of some subliminal messaging experiment? Did I eat something that has made me prone to hyper-imaginative episodes? Has someone's generosity recently rubbed me the wrong way, irritating me on a subconscious level?

Scanning through my memories, I try to find any reasonable shred of evidence to substantiate these conjectures. I come up with nothing. And with no plausible explanation, I'm at a loss for what

I can do at this point besides wait this out in the hopes it will all subside. Should I call my metaphysiologist? Get some rest?

Then it occurs to me that there is one minor thing I can do: I can at least ask you if these scenes are at all realistic or just sheer fantasy. As a generosity manager, you would know, and that would help me figure out if this is something I'm completely imagining or if it has some basis in reality, perhaps in past experiences or snippets of news I may have seen and forgotten.

From across the living room, you look at me with wide eyes, the final unnerving stage in the transformation my inquiry has been rendering upon you.

In the past several minutes, you've gone from recumbent across the full length of the sofa to seated upright, almost at the edge of the left cushion, like you were trying to get as close to me as you could without leaving the couch.

Still reclining in the lounge chair by the patio door, I become nervous, driven by your body language to suspect that my situation is dire or highly peculiar. I brace myself for some bad news. But when your words finally come, they baffle me.

"How do you know what I did this past week?"

"What do you mean?" I ask, not following at all.

"All the things you've just described are related to the clients I've been working with. Those situations are scenarios we've set up for observation or training."

"Whoa. Weird. I thought these were just random images related to generosity. I have no idea where they came from. I just wanted to know if they were at all realistic or just utterly absurd."

"Well, now you know they're very real. It's what we do. The kind of thing I was just doing."

"Wow, I had no clue that *that's* what actually happens in your job."

"Yeah, it's very serious stuff."

"Is it, you know…"

My eyes flit over to our housewarming aloe plant, as if I'll find the right word there. Shifting my gaze only makes it easier to use the word I'd had in mind. I go with it and finish posing my question.

"Hard? Treating generosity like that can't be fun."

"No, rest assured, it's *far* from fun," you answer quietly.

My eyes come back to you as you continue.

"I'm not some sicko, and generosity management isn't about coming down harsh on aberrant generosity. But you know how powerful generosity can be. You have to exert very firm control."

"But how do you do it? Are you just used to it?"

"Sort of. Maybe not surprisingly, this traces back to my childhood. I never told you about how, growing up, I despised generosity."

"Despised?" I repeat the word as if that will move it to some part of the room where its incongruity with your personality can be reconciled with its possible role in the throng of scenes I witnessed during the colloquium.

"Yes, *despised*," you confirm. "You see, I lived in a neighborhood where generosity was encouraged and trusted but not guided, not disciplined. Always freely roaming and prodding us to do things.

"Typically, acts motivated by generosity were underwhelming and mismatched, even inappropriate to the need. But even so, they placated or delighted the recipients, because who wouldn't be glad to receive some kind of assistance or care? And no obvious harm was being done. But later, some trends became clear to me. People were often pulled by their generosity into situations where their skills weren't applicable or their inexperience would bungle things. Or they would give time, effort, money, or things to endeavors, but insufficiently. Or they would give too much of the wrong thing."

I nod, recalling times generosity pushed me to say yes to Qalixy when I should have said no.

"So while this would help and encourage the recipients in the short term, issues cropped up later. The recipients would expect or hope for more assistance, which they never got or didn't get enough of. Many failed in their endeavors and blamed themselves, wondering how they could fail after receiving the good will of others. A crude analogy could be, if you were starving and I came along and gave you cartons of candy bars, you'd be somewhat better off. But in the end, your problem hasn't really been solved, and the pseudo-solution has its own problems."

Your words come at me faster and faster, which I take to be reflective of the pace at which ideas are entering your consciousness.

"Maybe down the road, when you have cavities and other issues like chronic hyperglycemia, you don't make the connection and think you should have brushed more diligently or exercised more often. Or maybe you do make the connection, but you don't want to be ungrateful. Giving out shoddy freebies to people who need real resources—only glibly, partially solving a problem— that is just patronizing in the end and obstructs sustainable progress. There were also cases of generosity driving people to give more than they should have. I remember Mr. Norolian would *always* be helping us with math homework in the afterschool center, but he really should have been using that time to do cardio for the sake of improving his memory. We found out about that after the fact, a couple years later, when we heard he had been put on anti-amnesia medication. It had nasty side effects, but that's preferable to memory loss."

You go quiet as you scratch the scars on your heart, which have become itchy once again. You take on this look of contentment, your face resembling that of a cat sunning itself on the sidewalk. I want to remind you to use the lotion I gave you, but I don't want to nag, especially in your moment of gratification. So instead

I gaze out the window at the observatory atop Kaleidoscope Mountain, at the sizzle of summer sunlight on its geodesic glass dome.

When the silence has gone on for a while, I assume you're done giving the backstory. But the moment I'm about to ask how your typical client feels about your treatment of his or her generosity, you say, "So that's how I came to deplore generosity."

Your words pull my gaze back inside and prompt me to imagine myself as a young adult arriving at the same emotional state after being let down—both directly and vicariously—by generosity.

"Generosity seemed to just make people feel better about themselves," you continue. "It seemed to only affirm their agency, assure them that they *could* help out and contribute. Or generosity got people pulled into things that took them away from personal priorities.

"And I thought, if that's what generosity is for, there's no way I'm going to trust it, much less follow it. So I resisted people's generosity. My attitude became unwelcoming, and whenever generosity approached, I'd shoo it away. And I suppressed mine, kept it locked away and starved for attention. Maybe then I was a sicko. Misguided by fear. I was afraid that I'd hurt others and myself if I were swayed by my generosity. Only much later did I find out that generosity requires discernment to be effective, for us to have more meaningful relationships with it. Then I realized that's what we'd been missing all along. Generosity has a natural tendency to notice and jump at opportunities to help, to get our attention and push us to act. But its discernment needs to be honed. How strongly it responds must be tempered."

"What about me and the people I grew up with? My generosity has only gotten me into trouble a few times, and I can't think of any stories that quite fit what you've described."

"You were lucky. Your generosity *was trained*. By the examples set by others' generosity. It acquired that discernment implicitly over time. You see, where I grew up, there just wasn't *any* good role model to follow. So our generosities were just doing what their instincts led them to. And that's what I see at work all the time. Stunted judgment, overzealousness, impatience, franticness. That's what you've been seeing in your mind today. Generosity just doing what it's mistakenly learned, when it doesn't know any better. You've also seen our attempts to overcome that."

I find myself nodding incessantly, the compulsive motion seeming necessary to digest everything you've been saying.

"So how did you first find out about generosity management?" I ask.

"Oh, you know how I was studying to be a chronographist. In that field, there's some serious generosity, and I saw for the first time ever how generosity could be keenly focused. To say I was impressed only begins to describe it."

And from there, our conversation goes on and on, in a rhythm of my questions followed by your answers. You explain what methods and equipment you use, how clients find you or vice versa, how their lives have changed through generosity management practices, why this is all still controversial.

As the sky gets very dark, we still have no idea how I ended up getting these glimpses into your line of work. But now I have a much clearer idea of what it is you do and what you believe are the roles of generosity in our lives and our society. And it becomes clear that you put a lot into your work, give a lot to your clients, for a salary that's far from glamorous. There lies the one thing, however, that I do not gain clarity on, that I do not ask about. Is this your own generosity at work? Does it pull you into the rescue of its kin? How far do you follow its lead?

Leaving the Chrysalis

When all that's left of the bagels are crumbs and memories and the lingering taste of pumpernickel and scallions in our mouths, that's when you say, "I have to tell you something," so seriously that I start to worry you got fired or are embroiled in some kind of crisis.

Before I can come up with any other speculations to dread, you say, "I'm not... actually a size G," like it's some afterthought or inconsequential preference or quirk.

"*What?*" I blurt, hoping that I heard you wrong or that there's some silver-lining twist to this.

"Size-G ideas don't fit me well. They're too large and too ambitious. I just can't fill them out and can't use them that effectively. I'm really size C," you say, making the situation unequivocal.

Still, I resist this revelation.

"No, that's not true," I say automatically, like it is a reflex of mine to use this phrase for seizing control of reality, for taking the nature of truth into my possession.

"I think I know my own mind and ideas well enough to assess fit," you reply, wresting jurisdiction over reality from me with your words.

"But size-G ideas have worked so well for you."

As I say this, everything else feels like it's falling away from us—as if the table between us with our plates, the chair I'm sitting on, your ever-familiar kitchen all around us—all of that is receding into another world, a reality we are no longer part of—leaving just us and this conversation.

"I could convincingly make size-G ideas work because there was a lot of size-C 'padding' beneath," you explain with air quotes.

"There's nothing wrong with layering," I try to assure you, even though I, along with many in our clique, have frowned upon it.

"Even so, there's considerable distance between me and the size-G ideas. So there's even more distance between me and the people and situations those ideas are in contact with. It almost always feels awkward."

I imagine you insulated by layers of ideas in our past conversations, me oblivious to how far away you were, how muffled our intellectual sparring must have felt to you.

"Wow," is all I can respond with.

Seconds of silence ooze by, until I can finally add, "But size-G ideas always seemed so becoming—always appeared to suit you well."

"Yes, 'appeared...' 'seemed,'" you echo, air quotes again, for attribution this time. You give me a moment to acclimate.

"I thought about donating my size-G ideas," you then say.

No! I want to shriek, but before I can, you continue.

"I'd rather you have them though. You're so fond of these ideas, and we've had such good times with them. And if having my size-G ideas as mementos is too troublesome, I know you'll find good homes for them and give my ideas to minds who will benefit from all that these ideas can equip them to do."

I stare at you, struggling to extrapolate the future you've initiated for yourself, for us. There will be no more sparring, no more deep dives into the wellsprings of inquiry or outings to swanky, cerebral galas thrown by the local erudites, no more expeditions to scale new peaks of knowledge and reason, no more forging of molten possibilities, no launching of ourselves through conceptual rifts.

So just *what* is it that we'll be doing together now? Sitting around like this, in banal conversation? Meeting up to bake casseroles and scones? Passively letting entertainment wash over us?

You are relinquishing—*undoing*—the very ties between us. I never thought about this—never had to—but without size-G ideas, there is no us. All our time together is comprised of interactions made possible by size-G ideas. There will be nothing left.

Saying no more, you shed your size-G ideas, letting go of how I've always known you. But you don't offer these ideas to me, don't hold them out to me as I expect you to.

Then I realize that I haven't yet agreed to take your ideas. I wonder if I should reach out for them, to accept them from you now.

But you just look at me with not even a hint of expectation in your eyes or in your posture. You sit there, serene but alert, your mind wrapped in the size-C ideas that lay beneath the G layer you've just pulled away. Knit tightly and intricately together, the ideas gleam as I consider them. The contours are familiar, paralleling those of the G. Hugging the features of your mind, they reveal your insecurities and regrets.

Amid the ideas, a very familiar one attracts my attention: the awareness of our human heritage, the fact that we are animals ever reinvented by environmental happenstance, social forces, and our ingenuity, noble when confidently humble. Imaginatively, I overlay upon it the corresponding size-G idea of yours that I've come to know so well: the narrative that we are descendants of those who dared to steal from lions, of those who molded wolves into dogs; the heirs of a legacy unparalleled by that of any other species ever to roam this planet, risen to be the champions of cosmic potential. That idea would never have revealed the doubts and humility that this size-C idea so clearly embraces. I see now that you are delighted by but ambivalent about our identity as humans. It is an honest bewilderment I would never have guessed was quintessential to you.

I look beyond this idea to find that the sophistication and reach of the C ideas are, of course, more limited yet surprisingly capable. You look like you'll be able to withstand the tumult of ideation storms, maneuver in light philosophical discourse, and actually be even more spry in dreams and fantasies.

This could work. You're still you. All the more so now, I'm starting to see. I just need to understand who I can now be with you.

Dreamscape

Tired out by the day, by constantly putting theory of mind into practice, I forget to take out my mind's eye contact lens before bed.

Then, in my dreams, I make my way through rooms and into woods that are crisp with cognitive clarity, conceptual detail beyond compare. I don't just see walls or trees but copper siding and rose concrete, blue spruce and young cedar. If this were any other dream, all the elements of the setting would be hazy, generically indistinct. But this time, everything feels comprehensible, explainable. All backstory knowable to me if I just look closely enough for history to reveal itself.

Under the foliage of aspens planted a century ago as atonement for decades of rampant logging, I walk a path, freshly wood-chipped by the town's ecological management division, to the zero-gravity zone.

When I'm nearing the end of this alleyway of aspens, I see you heading towards me.

"It's *you*," I blurt, my voice feeling like my voice and not like dream telepathy. "And it always has been you."

"So you recognize me this time," you reply, smiling through every word.

"Yes, I knew it was you so instantly that I'm embarrassed I didn't know all those other times."

"Well, my appearance does change from dream to dream and even during dreams."

In your voice there's that slight viscosity, stickiness even, that hints at the deliberateness with which you form your words.

"But your essence doesn't change. You feel the same. Your overall concept is the same. I can see that now."

"Right, but you have to notice that. Which isn't always easy."

I nod. I have a track record of not taking notice of the elements comprising my dreams.

"Anyways, forget the zero-gravity zone," you say. "There's somewhere else we should go."

You lead me down unmarked trails, moving so briskly that I can only catch glimpses of the details. The tatters of papery flakes hanging from branches we pass are all that remains of the wasp nests eliminated for the safety of children who commute along these paths to school. Under tall red pines, the needle litter is thick beneath our feet; the swirling gales a couple weeks ago have furnished this new plush carpeting.

From the tops of the hills we climb, I'm seeing this dream world as if in hindsight, from the future. Is this how you see this landscape too? Like it's all part of the past, settled into its place in history?

Then we're walking out upon a granite precipice, and you tell me, "Here it is," opening your arms to an expanse of intricate, colorful patterns and textures, like this part of the dream landscape has been modeled after a vast, thriving coral reef.

"It's actually everywhere, but this is where you can most clearly see it," you add.

It takes me a moment to figure out what I'm looking at. Particular portions are clearly facets of human psychology, cultural development, and scientific advancement—our ability to think abstractly, our love of storytelling, the creation of monetary systems, the invention of chronography, the discovery of emotional lensing—but the overall sweep of it isn't immediately obvious.

And then it is.

"The comprehension of who we are, of humanity," I murmur.

"Yes, it's what you've been building. What we're all building. This is what our dreams are really about," you say, pride glowing softly in your words.

I'm impressed by this capability of ours to engage in the ongoing self-diagnosis of the human condition. We can perform this for ourselves, not needing to wait for an outside intelligence to do so for us, to provide us this perspective and its insights.

Then something troubling gets my attention. Wide swaths and densely packed pockets in the structure are hideous. Avarice, hatred, violence, contempt, exploitation. And though I am capable of perceiving them with greater granularity, I choose to not to consider their heartbreaking, infuriating particulars and instead keep them at the level of generalities.

You follow my upset gaze with your own placid one.

"Yes, that too is who we are," you confirm.

They are almost disgusting beyond comprehension, but through the contact lens, I can acknowledge that these facets of us are utterly logical when seen in the full breadth of human history, in the context of the environments and forces that have shaped us. There is probably no way we would have made it here without them.

Then I wake up, my mind sore from perceiving all the conceptual detail. Amid the jumble of throbbing thought fragments is an intuition gleaming with the promise of meaning. With my head heavy on my pillow, I will that intuition into focus, and it expands into an awareness that I can only have now that I'm awake: that the construction of this grand view of ourselves will never be complete. And that's what makes it all worthwhile.

I smile and pluck away the contact lens, overdue for removal.

Then I reach for the phone to call in sick to work.

In the Care of Others

When I step into your living room, all the pictures on the walls stun me. I nearly lose my grasp on the watering can. Its handle starts slipping down my loosening fingers. I feel gravity tug insistently at the watering can's fullness and tighten my grip. Then my attention returns to the walls. The images cover the wood paneling like a lattice of memories, arraying before me pieces of the past like I've stepped into your hippocampus. They impel me to rethink my conception of your relationship with your self. They won't let me budge until I do.

Since I first met you, you've entrusted the care of your self to others. Back then, it was the conservatory, now it's the academy. Prior to that was the discovery center, and before that the enrichment program. You seem to prefer having your self in controlled environments for balanced, disciplined cultivation, and this arrangement means being out of touch with your self for long periods of time. Only on some weekends do you make the hours-long drive to the academy's campus to go out to lunch and talk with your self.

Being in each other's company for longer than an afternoon, that is limited to the vacations you take with your self in the winter and summer. You always book some kind of trip for just the two of you during these seasons. You've told me that you want to treat your self; to give your self a dramatic change of setting from the campus buildings and same old city streets and familiar neighborhoods; to give your self the chance to see, do, and think about new, exciting things. But I've always thought that you make travel plans because you wouldn't know what to do with your self without an itinerary, without some kind of structure, without some sort of distractive setting full of easy conversation starters or full-on substitutes for conversation. I simply assumed that you feel the need to place the two of you in locales where many facets of the landscape are ripe for the attentional picking, like that's the prerequisite for being alone with your self.

Those travels always start awkwardly, you've said. At first, it's all about relearning how to be comfortable with your self. But then, there in breezy oceanside towns, cities dense with convivial culture, country valleys of fragrant sunlight, and deserts rich with exotic geology, it's easy to indulge your self with paella and dumplings, concerts and plays, snorkeling and canoeing, snowshoeing and caving, paper-making and castle tours. Freshly encountered places, plants, and people can rapidly fill the sketchbooks you have a habit of giving your self, the intently focused drawing keeping your self occupied for hours on end. You can both feel at ease. Be almost as comfortable as you feel when you're away from your self. A comfort I could never feel.

"I don't know how you do it," I've said to you over pound cake and coffee. "I'd miss my self too much."

But maybe, I've sometimes considered when we've had these conversations, I'm too protective of—too attached to—my self. Could I ever entrust my self to others the way you do?

"I do miss her, but I don't have the time or qualifications to do all the training and teaching," you've answered over gingersnaps and tea.

I've wondered if it's really time or actually interest. Maybe you don't have time because you've engineered your schedule that way, packing it full of work because you're more interested in that than in your self.

Now all this needs to be mentally reworked; the material of my thoughts must be re-molded.

Now that I see photos of her smiling face and her pencil drawings of birds and crayon-rendered landscapes—beaches at sunset, hills topped with castles and forts, glaciers gleaming in the sunlight, treehouses of a jungle village—now that I'm surrounded by pictures of and by your self here in your living room, the picture in my mind of you and your self is recalled for revision. It's still a case of responsibility transfer, but the motivation could be completely different from what I've thought.

There seem to be two probable reasons for what I'm seeing here.

3. My impressions were correct, and you have little interest in taking care of your self. But you feel pressured to be reminded of her, to put her in a place of prominence in your life, as is expected in our culture.
4. Or, more likely, you care deeply about your self, so deeply in fact that you want her to have what you think is the best care.

I don't have the time or qualifications to do all the training and teaching.

I had always focused on the "time" component of that explanation. The "qualifications" part seemed to me an afterthought, an easy, additional bit of rationalizing; who among us, after all, is highly qualified to take care of her self? None of us are born with the ability to fully look after our selves, and few of us pick up all the necessary skills from our families. All of us let our selves go from time to time and have to keep on working at our ability to care for our selves. We all have to rely on each other to keep our selves healthy. Perhaps if our schooling and society focused more on the care of our selves, people would have fantastically healthy relationships with their selves. In the absence of that, no one with our level of education is qualified to fully care for his or her self. So that piece of your explanation struck me as trite.

But now I think I get it. To you, all that matters tremendously. Since none of us excel at self-care right off the bat, you'd rather put your self in the care of those who have trained and gained years of experience in the caring of the self. You're afraid of letting your self down, of being inadequate, of failing to fulfill the responsibility of helping her mature and stay healthy. So you'd rather transfer this responsibility to others. The vacations and sketchbooks and afternoon walks—those are things you know you can get right for her. So you stick to that. Just that.

But the self is not easily satisfied by such limited relationships. She will no doubt push you to get to know her better and demand that you care for her, especially as she, gaining more and more maturity, grows to take greater care of you. I'm certain of this because when I look closely at her artwork, you are in many of the scenes, captured in charcoal or pastel or graphite or watercolor, even if only blurrily or gesturally. That must be part of her process for thinking through how you fit—or don't—into the culture, the space, the events, and circumstances around you.

Life too will demand your increased participation. Situations will arise that aren't easily accommodated by the limited patterns of interaction you've become ensconced in with your self, and those situations will shove you both out of the narrow confines of that compact repertoire of rapport. It will probably happen little by little. And it probably has already been happening—is probably happening during the very vacation you are on now with your self.

If you really listen to each other, there's still time to retake and excel at the responsibility you have ceded. You are in the centers of each other's attention. You just need to more fully be there.

For a moment, I wonder if there's more I can do to help besides just watering the plants while you're away. But then I'm sure that if there were something, it wouldn't really be necessary.

Confidant

In today's mail is a postcard from your self. And the moment you recognize the handwriting on it as the cursive lettering you perfected with her now fluidly forming words like *the* and *strawberry*, when you know it could be from no one else, you flip over the postcard, to avoid reading any more, to deny her message entry into your mind.

Your head recoils a little as the close-up of a sunlion on the opposite side startles you. You haven't seen one for years, and it reminds you of her, of her affinity for gorgeous, ferocious animals. While preferable to her words, the picture of the majestic grasslands beast provokes you to put the postcard in the pile of unwanted catalogs and pamphlets.

But you know you'd eventually feel guilty if you discarded this small message that has traveled hundreds of miles (actually thousands, according to the postmark you don't look at in detail) to end up in your hands. So you give it to me, so that it will be out of the home you've made without her and in the care of someone you trust to keep but never mention it.

After handing me the little envelope you've placed it in—to prevent any further incidental reading of the postcard—you tell me, "If you want to, you can read it. I don't mind. You know my self, after all."

The way you say this implies—acknowledges—that I was going to read it, with or without your approval, as soon as I got the chance.

But I manage to go several days without withdrawing the postcard from its snug, plain white envelope. It sits on my bookshelf, in front of the spines of texts that have molded my thoughts into understandings, waiting, like it is only a matter of time before it joins their ranks.

Then, on Thursday evening, on the train ride home, I see a woman holding a little portion of a beach in her left hand, the tiny fragments of waves lapping the strip of tan sand on her palm. She's just diagonally across the aisle, in the row of seats ahead of me on the left. The bit of beach sways slightly to and fro as the train rocks our bodies with its eagerness to run its route. The landscape fragment in her hand strikes me as exactly the kind of beach the four of us stood upon together years ago, when we felt poised to head into the future.

I want to talk with this woman, to ask her about her philosophy on life over coffee or better yet, brunch on Tuesday. And I really want to read the postcard.

Slowly I pull the postcard from the envelope. Once I've got half of it out, the sunlion's huge, sharp eyes stare intensely at the ceiling as I finish sliding the postcard from its paper sheath. This massive predator's mane blazes outward in all directions, the orange corona of a face aglow with fine golden fur. For a while, I just hold the postcard, my gaze lingering on the sunlion, like I'm studying his expression through a two-way mirror that keeps him unaware of my presence.

Though you've sanctioned it, I'm not completely comfortable with this textual eavesdropping I'm about to engage in. It's a only modest intrusion upon her privacy but still an intrusion. But I want to know that she's all right and to gain some glimpse of what she's doing and thinking out there.

I turn over the postcard. My eyebrows rise. It's not an update on how she's doing, not a reminder of who you were and could be again, not an inspiring anecdote or well-wishing note. It's a recipe for berry scones. That's all.

So I walk out into the crisp late-October night, to go buy the ingredients, to bake some of these scones tomorrow. What else can I do? I get honey, flour, blueberries and strawberries, thanking the bodega cashier with extra courtesy, as if the success of the scones might rest entirely on her whims.

In the morning, my well-rested eyes slowly follow the path her purple pen took around the back of the postcard, until I'm fully acquainted with the recipe. Then in my kitchen, where autumnal sunlight soaks into countertops and cupboard doors, I carefully measure out the ingredients, wanting to get it right, achieve the taste and texture intended by your self. Once everything is appropriately proportioned, I mix the ingredients in a large ceramic bowl with a wooden spoon. As the dough they form thickens, my forearm becomes sore, a sign that I am out of practice, a reminder that I haven't baked much besides casserole since Qalixy left.

After the dough reaches a nice consistency, I drop it on the corner of the counter I've dusted with flour for this next step. I shape the dough into two rounds, the first of which I divide into wedges with my one long, thin spatula. I then cut into the second numerous times at odd angles. Giving each plenty of space, I arrange all these pieces on two baking sheets.

As they sit in the dense heat of the oven, the sweet, bready aroma of the baking scones eases my mind, offers me the reassurance I've yearned for. If she has time to bake and eat scones, she must be doing all right.

We'll eat them this afternoon. I won't tell you the recipe is from her, like it's a secret between me and her. And one day it will be. I will keep this secret to share with her.

Or will you be able to determine the origin of these scones as you chew the first bite? Through that way only you can know your self even with all the years and miles between the two of you, will you know this recipe is meant for you?

Either way, the scones will be delicious.

Who You Wish To Be

E

Our little summer-afternoon outing winds down with the three of us positioned lazily on a quaint collage of four small, square picnic blankets in our usual urban meadow, me fully recumbent, you sitting cross-legged, she laying on her side, head propped up with her left hand.

"*Oh,*" I hear from her direction.

I'm not sure if she's said something or just sighed. I tentatively decipher this murmuring as hopeful and wistful.

With her gaze resting on you, she says, "I want you to be the next me."

This remark makes me think that a sitcom or movie or her is being produced and that she wants you to play her in the next season or sequel.

You look at her quizzically, then at me. Meeting your gaze, I raise my eyebrows just a little, as if to shrug with my eyes.

"You mean you want me to take over your life? Work your job and hang out with your friends?" you ask her.

"No, no. Well, I do feel like sometimes I need a vacation from being me," she answers. "But I kind of meant the opposite... I should have said, 'I want the next me to be you'—like you."

I know she's got this all worked out in her mind but has to wrangle the wording.

"I think she's trying to say that who she's going to become in the near future should have the qualities she's observed and admires in you," I offer, to reduce the awkwardness.

"Yes, that's about right," she agrees.

"Wow, that's such a compliment," you reply, your voice uncharacteristically soft and slow. Clearly you're touched.

With her confirmation of my interpretation followed by your reaction, there's a twinge in my heart, a hurting mixture of jealousy and feeling left out. She's never paid me any compliment of such magnitude, and while I may not be role model material, I'd like to think that all the times I've been there for her count for something as significant as this admiration she's having difficulty articulating.

I almost expect you to blush, but you almost never do. My cheeks, on the other hand, do grow hot, like I'm blushing for you, taking up the role of your stand-in emoter. But really, I'm embarrassed by my reaction to her sentiments, by being wounded by her high regard for you. I never thought I'd be this insecure, needing more validation to be around a friend who excels at being a friend and at being a person.

H

On the 2-burner electric stove in your cozy hallway kitchenette, you cook us a 3-dish dinner, this display of your culinary abilities only fanning the flames of her esteem for you. Maybe more like dousing that emotional blaze with a kerosene of desirable practical ability.

The fragrance of hot garlic wafts all around us as she and I sit just a few feet from you, on the floor of the adjoining 5-tatami room.

"The tropical landscape painting by Mïltazé really surprised me," I mention as my contribution to our collective reflection on today's visit to the culture forum's gallery.

"It had colors I've never seen in any of her other works," I add. "I thought she only painted the boreal landscapes of her homeland."

"Yeah, that one painting, definitely *surprising*. Looking at it made me really aware of where artists work," she says. "Especially since the description by the painting said she was trying to capture the chromatic essence of the equatorial island she was visiting. And as I thought a little more about where artists created their work, the gallery was no longer just a room with art hanging on the walls. I saw it as an array of windows upon landscapes of the past. Then it struck me that the gallery would be better described as a collection of windows that each offers a glimpse into the mind of its painter. That got me thinking that when we're looking at paintings, we're standing roughly where the painters were when they created these pieces of art, and beyond the canvases were landscapes now absent. All that's left for us as the audience is this piece of art."

"Interesting," you murmur, stirring the string beans in the wok.

All that's audible for a while is the sizzling of these vegetables in safflower oil.

Then you say, "So if you think about a painting or drawing as being a record of the picture plane, when we look at a painting, it's like we're looking at a slice of space and time as rendered by a painter."

"Yes!" she exclaims. "We're looking at this thing that was connected to both the painter and the landscape, and it is all that remains. Or at least it's all we have as the audience. What lay on opposite sides of the painting and is implied by the painting, those are now gone—with the painting the remaining artifact."

"I've never really thought about it that way," I consider aloud. "Maybe because I don't paint. But it is wild to consider the space and time and their inhabitants that are... implied by the painting, to use your words. Those are all distant from us as a present-day audience. It's like the painting comes from and reminds us of a reality that's long gone."

She nods heartily, perhaps with the satisfaction that she has contributed an intriguingly new perspective to my thoughts.

"I've never thought this way either," you agree. "Maybe because it's harder to think about other art forms this way. Because the media they're cast in are more... distant from their artists. Like in the case of novels, we aren't reading off the paper or computer the author wrote on. Or when we're watching a film, we aren't looking at the actual materials that stood between artist and subject, the medium where their artistic relationship has been consummated. We could, in the case of film, have some consideration of what the cameraman and director saw and think about what happened on both sides of the camera, but we're not in contact with the actual medium with which they worked, be it spools of film or bits of data. We're numerous steps and intermediates, even duplications away from the materials the filmmakers used."

I nod, wondering what this means for our relationships. When we have in hand the pages of a letter once held by the sender, when we're on the same side of the paper as the writer once was but on the other end of the message, is there some immediacy and intimacy potentially afforded by that physicality I've so automatically overlooked? Something that I haven't noticed the absence of in emails and blurbles?

And what if *we* are each like those letters and paintings? Here in your apartment, I sit at a distance from you where at various times stood your parents, teachers and others who shaped the course of your life. Am I on "the other side" of them now, seeing who you are now but not the contributors to—the influences "behind"—this person you have become? Perhaps here I am not on the other side of a canvas but on the other side of time, the half of your life that contains the present.

That contains these moments that are now quiet with communal thoughtfulness.

K

She walks to the train station with jaunty steps, as if she were a morning person at 7 a.m. My pace is sluggish and I lag behind her like a non-morning person at 7, no 6 a.m. The exhaustion from our afternoon slacklining is really hitting me. The evening glow from the sun hanging just below the horizon keeps me energized enough to keep moving. I'll have a harder time making it the rest of the way home, once I've stepped off the train and into my residential neighborhood lit with only the occasional streetlight.

The chirping of crickets and cicadas oscillates between lulling me to sleep and keeping me awake. It reminds me of the times Zona would talk to me as we lay in our beds at opposite ends of the room. I could just let my consciousness dissolve in the cadence and consonance of her words, but I would also want to consider the meaning they formed, the snippets of life they rendered. She made me sleepier and want to be more alert.

"If only I could be like *that*," she says, seemingly daydreaming aloud.

Coming from a few steps ahead of me, her words seem to refer to something down the street that I haven't seen or come across yet.

"Then I could finally help you in the ways you need," she continues. "Do for you some of what you've done for me."

I'm taken aback, stunned by this aspiration for her future self. Am I really deserving of the benefits of her desired transformation?

I smile at that thought. Now it's me who has paid you a compliment.

Perceptions of Proximity

We're riding a cable car down the length of Wotoz canyon, you and I its sole passengers through a summery landscape of flowing water, shear rock, trees and sunlight. The serene surroundings have mesmerized us into a tranquil silence. But now, your gaze turns from the cable car windows and again returns to the answer to my existential pensiveness, the unabating need to find or create deep meaning. You've been looking at it repeatedly, episodically ever since we met at the cable car station. It's looming right in front of but remains invisible to me. You can't make out the details, but you know it has something to do with acceptance and family. Its nearness and imposing stature command your attention, as it will mine when I get closer to it, when it collides into my consciousness. You try to determine if its location is changing, if it is inching towards me or drifting away.

In the edge of my peripheral vision, I see you staring in that way you often do. Your eyes have taken on that preoccupied intensity they always have when you see how close people are to answers, for questions that have become well articulated or for questions that have yet to gain verbal or even mental substance.

"You know how close I am to an answer," I conclude aloud, turning my head to look directly at you.

"Yes," you reply reluctantly.

The low, flat tone of your voice makes it clear that your terse reply is all you want to say about the matter. With only slight difficulty and hesitation, I let quietness engulf us again. I know how reticent you are about the answers you see.

"You're just about there," you want to blurt, but you're afraid that then I won't go as far as I can—that I'll only see and grasp part of the answer if I know that I'm close.

I try to read your still-enthralled gaze, gauge from it how close this answer is. The handful of estimates that I've attempted so far have all missed the mark drastically. Like that time when we were standing on the forestgazing platform jutting out of Mt. Vloris. I was sure you were looking at someone on the verge of being hit by the answer she so needed. I was also way off about what your reaction would be.

You were suddenly no longer listening to me expound upon the need for more responsible consumption of scientific knowledge. In your consciousness, the power balance of your sensory modalities had undergone a complete shift, with vision rapidly and fully privileged over hearing, your eyes transfixing upon the space in front of a girl sitting on the edge of the viewing platform. Abandoning my tirade, falling silent, I followed your gaze to her, that smartly dressed adolescent.

Judging from where your eyes appeared to be focused and how intensely they peered at that point in space, I inferred that some important answer was right there, staring her in the face. I thought then her mood might suddenly go from a relaxed mindfulness of place to the rapture of insight or the shock of stunning realization.

To me, she appeared small, dwarfed by the backdrop of large mountains and even larger clouds; her lanky, mid-growth-spurt form seemed to be reaching into an impossibly gargantuan world, in which all her pastel linen and seersucker would be inevitably overwhelmed amid forest and sky. But for you, she had a vividness, a sharp chromaticity completely absent in the surroundings enveloping her.

"Sorry," you murmured to me, still peering at her. "It's just that she's a ways off from a small but critical answer about her past," you explained. "And she's about to turn her attention else-where. She might be ready to give up, at least for now."

And I became keenly aware that with your cognitive far-sightedness, you can see distant ideas with as much as ease as the rest of us see the ideas that are within grasp.

"Do you want to talk with her?" I asked.

"Yes and no. I don't know what I should say to her."

Your words acutely reminded me of my sporadic desperation to reconcile the dubious decisions of my past self with the con-science of my present self. I knew that if I were you, and I didn't talk with this girl, my future self would surely regret this ceding of the agency I have here. I didn't want you to be afflicted by that regret in the coming weeks—or years. So my mind labored furious-ly to determine what you could say to her, what words wouldn't be too intrusive and stood some reasonable chance of being helpful. I wanted so much for us to combine forces, together move her to-wards a vital epiphany and you away from regret. If only I could come up with the right words, everything would work out.

Abruptly you turned your attention back to me, and as your eyes flitted over me quickly but carefully, the grip of some sur-prise closed tightly upon you.

"Distract me," you told me, these two words quiet and firm, abrupt and jarring.

Your words impelled me to take some kind of action, and then the intensity of your eyes indicated that an answer we both needed had to be right before us. Then, without any thought, I brought my hand to yours and squeezed my fingers around your palm. The warmth of your hand gently astounded me. And the worlds around and within us condensed to a single one consisting only of us.

Steadily, the cable car continues along its way. While the tips of the branches around us slowly sweep elliptically, as if caressing the humid air, you continue that custom we've established.

Before I can transform the wideness and brightness of your eyes into an estimation of distance, you wrap my hand within yours. Then it doesn't matter how close or far I am from this answer.

The Volatility of
Peer-to-Peer Lending

Dazed with dejection engendered by the harsh critiques of my identity managers—who are now demanding more compartmentalization, among other things—I somehow wind up at your doorstep with a box of butter cake in hand. You usher me into the kitchen and immediately brew up some coffee for us.

"You need to have some confidence in me," you tell me after we've eaten the dense, flaky pastry.

"But I already do," I reply, puzzled, wondering if you've gambled it all away.

"No, I mean confidence in me that's for *you*. I really appreciate the confidence you've placed in me for me, but it can't help you as directly in situations like this."

"Oh, I see. A self-esteem cache. Like the stash of secret accomplishments in your closet."

"Yes, exactly."

"All right, I'm all for it."

And it works. Brilliantly. In your company, my spirits are lifted by my confidence in you. Whenever I see you, whatever mood I am in is instantly improved. Happiness turns to joy, cynicism becomes pragmatism, doubt diminishes to make room for hope and reason.

Until my confidence in you is seemingly gone. When I'm around you, I am no longer emboldened. I no longer feel that bright, buoyant energy. I'm just left to tread in murky unease.

And it's not just my confidence in you. It's also your confidence in yourself. It's now you who feels better around me, your confidence in me lifting you out of insecurity. I know you know I know. So I wait for you to tell me what's wrong.

But a week goes by, and you volunteer not even a hint. I have to ask you what happened.

You look out your kitchen window at the air streaked with raindrops, considering my question, like you never expected me to pose it.

"So there's this girl," you begin. "She did a real number on me."

You say nothing more, so I imagine her as having the discreet superpower of sapping confidence, debilitating her foes with uncertainty and diminished agency. Your silence continues on, leaving me little choice but to attempt a rudimentary recapitulation to jumpstart your stalled explanation.

"You meet a girl, and years of accruing confidence are nullified? What, is she a hypnotist or ruthlessly critical?"

"No, she's actually nice. Too nice. And before I knew it, all my confidence was gone. I just felt inadequate. But it's been lovely."

"All the confidence you had was negated, and you liked it?"

"You'd have to meet her to understand."

"Okay, where can I find her?"

"She's a regular at the reflectorium. She's usually by the autumn window."

So the following afternoon, I'm there, and so is she. She gazes out into a landscape of yellowing ginkgoes. She has the look of a cloud watcher caught between acceptance and imagination, between seeing clouds as they are and turning them into puffy renditions of animals or objects.

With the mug of coffee I've just purchased, I approach her and, at the risk of forfeiting my freshly rebuilt confidence, ask if

I may join her. She waves an open hand at the vacant seat across from her.

The topic of cognitive organization comes up after she mentions one of her hobbies is cultivating prototypes for subordinate-level categories.

"Because if you don't structure the hierarchies of thought, you know who will," she says.

"Yes, I know who and what will," I reply. "But it took a while to understand that. It's not trivial. Wouldn't you rather shortcut that process of discovery for others?"

"If they see that as desirable," she says, nodding.

From there, our conversation goes on into the topics of foraging for identity capital and cataloguing wasted time. Her thoughtful words reveal her to be personable and graciously intelligent, so much so that I have to wonder if she is expertly skilled in making impressions or is highly empathetic toward those of us who did not have the benefit of being prodigies. Fleetingly, I imagine you running your fingertips over the impression she has left upon your psyche, feeling the curves of the indentations.

My confidence doesn't vaporize as I had feared. But now I can conjecture upon what happened to yours.

Her words seem to hint that within her thoughts lies the answer to some cosmic question. Or that she at least knows what the question is, knows how language can be concisely used to most meaningfully and unequivocally inquire about a deep, existential truth.

You must have felt this way too. But unlike you, I don't trust this intuition. I don't place any confidence in this feeling that tugs at my psyche, that could easily become a belief, that has become a belief in your mind and sequestered away your confidence. I choose to instead interpret the tone of her voice as indicating that her cognitive style is heavily integrationist.

And the convivial conversation continues on, perhaps foregoing some connection to a grand insight into the nature of reality, while definitely validating my esteem for humanity.

As if we are the emissaries of our dreams' better provinces, convening here to extend their reach.

Caloric Contrivance

My bare arms break out in goosebumps. It feels like a cold breeze is wafting by. Like someone has just opened a freezer door. Like those moments when you walk by a convenience store as some-one's coming out, and the air-conditioned air rushes out into the bright summer sunlight.

But it can't be either of those. We are far from refrigerators and air conditioners in this garden that smells faintly of lychee, and we are far from winter in the middle of July's thick heat.

"Did you feel that?" I ask, to confirm that the chill I felt has an existence beyond my physiology.

"Feel what?" you ask.

"That sudden coldness in the air. The brief drop in temperature."

"Oh," you murmur. "That's me. I forgot to put on my heart-warmer today. It was so hot when I left, I didn't even notice that I didn't have it on."

I had no idea you wore one. All this time, there's been this additional layer between us, helping you retain warmth and keep-ing your coldness from seeping into your surroundings.

Now it all makes sense. Why you're always drinking warm beverages and reading sentimental novels. Why you never get an-gry. And why...

"You're so reluctant to have a heart-to-heart with me or any-one," I blurt. "Because of this."

"Yes, that's one reason."

"But that's why you really need it," I hasten to tell you. "To bring your metaphysiology back to baseline."

"I don't think it would," you reply flatly.

"That's because you underestimate the warmth a heart can have," I assertively conclude, like I'm seizing authorship of your story. "But of course you would underestimate, because there's nothing to tell you otherwise. You're not getting close enough to anything warm enough to effectively warm you up."

"I don't think it's an issue of proximity or estimation. I've felt plenty of warmth. I remember how intense and nice it can be. I got to be this way because I was close to someone with cardiac hypothermia."

"What? But that's not contagious."

"Not in the conventional sense, but I grew to admire some of the symptoms I saw in my friend. The distant calm, the stability of comfortable detachment. It's like you're just naturally declining to board any and all emotional rollercoasters, then just watching the screaming riders rise and fall, free to simply—leisurely—observe from the comfort of solid ground. Like you're immune to the tumult of unnecessary drama around you. It never infected her, no matter how virulent. I also like how people sometimes treated her more seriously. And before I knew it, the temperature of my heart was going lower and lower."

"I can't believe I didn't know this," I say, voice just barely louder than a whisper. "I just thought your stolidness came from practicing meditation, or from an upbringing with very composed parents."

"Yes, I'm just warm enough to give you that impression. Usually."

The boulder beneath us begins to feel uncomfortable. I stand up.

If I didn't know better, perhaps I'd feel deceived or betrayed. But there was no malicious or selfish intent here. It's just you being who you are. Someone who likes having a low heart temperature, trying to keep it from falling too low, from adversely affecting people; someone who would, of course, never be compelled to explain that.

"So you see now," you say as if prompting me to look at some geological feature in the landscape. "As long as I like the idea of being cold-hearted, I probably will be."

I still think a heart-to-heart will change that. I think that once you feel it, you'll like the warmth you don't consciously know you miss. But I don't want to press the point. It wouldn't help even if I did. At most, I'd win an argument with you, my intellect contending with yours, in your arena sanitized of emotions, using facts and anecdotes to debate the nature of human metaphysiology. Neither of us really needs or wants that.

What I want is to grab you and thaw your heart with mine. But you would only push me away.

What I need to do is engineer a situation in which warmth is a necessity, the way it could never be in our comfortable, bustling urban environment. If there's to be any hope of adjusting the temperature of your psyche, I need to place us in a situation where warmth is unavoidably crucial. Like plunge you into the depths of space, where you would be debilitated by your condition, the darkness pin-pricked with light only made tolerable—ultimately survivable—by human warmth.

Then, when I look over at your aloof face, I've got it. Your foodie disposition. As my attention is then caught and held by a hummingbird nimbly flitting from cyania to cyania, reaching so precisely into each for nectar with its fine quill of a bill, the rough beginnings of a plan coalesce.

Inadequate Interventions

Turned hyper-frenetic by worry and insecurity, you launch into frantically multitasking your way through your to-do list. That doesn't go well. Your attention is jostled too easily and too rapidly, like it's some skittish animal constantly startled by any little sound or movement, constantly darting in different directions. You lurch from emails to bills, swerve from tidying up and organizing to planning out your schedule, veer from cleaning the bathroom to reviewing strategy reports.

I try to do my own work, to forge memories and distill patterns from the bulk of amassed data, but ultimately I am unable to focus and make any appreciable progress. I'm distracted by the atmosphere of panicky productivity you've created. But I leave it to you to figure out, hoping the tumult will subside once you've caught up with outstanding work.

But as you hack through chores and responsibilities, follow-ups and wrap-ups, you uncover more and more tasks and worries. All too soon, you're laboring late into the night, on the myriad things that lie on your desk and that pop into your mind, nibbling intermittently at a bar of dark chocolate. Until you finally go to bed out of exhaustion.

In the morning, you're calm and refreshed, until you catch sight of where you left off last night. You dive back into that fray of you versus uncompleted work. The hustle only comes to a halt when it's time to go to the office, where you then operate in the same unfocused, haphazard mode of panicked pseudo-productivity.

During your lunch break, you turn to checking off personal items from your to-do list. You go to the optometrist to order a new set of glasses, which you've been meaning to do for weeks now. On the way back, you get two dozen bagels to stock up for upcoming breakfasts, but more importantly, to have high-calorie foodstuffs handily available for your workathons.

Once back in the office, your task-juggling fervor resumes in full force.

As you enter into the third day of this, it's clear that the attempt to address earnest concerns has become an obsession with progress on all fronts. You devote every minute to misguided attempts to be productive. Not sure what to do, I take the only action I can think of: summon a sedationist. The best one that I can find and that we can afford. The one parents of the brattiest kids call during temper tantrums.

Impressively, she's shows up in a matter of minutes, brought over by her chauffeuring service. I let her in. Plainly dressed in khaki pants and a white linen shirt, she enters carrying a corduroy shoulder bag, her demeanor calming in its clearly manifested composure.

"Has there been any change since you called me?" she asks in a flowy voice.

"No, it's still more or less what I described," I answer.

"Okay, I'm going to leave my cat *Mulberry* here, and he'll join us if necessary," she tells me. "We'll start with the warm milk."

I nod at her words.

Then, looking me in the eyes, she asks, "No allergies, right?"

"Only to small talk," I answer.

"Great."

She places her bag on the floor, then crouches down to slowly lift from its interior a calico cat—*Mulberry*. After setting him down by her ankles, she takes a thermos from her bag.

Standing up, she nods at me, and we head up the spiral staircase to your home office. "There's someone here to see you," I tell you from the doorway.

Still huddled over the scattered papers on your desk, you reply hurriedly, "What? No! I need to finish these," unequivocally impatient to shoo her and me away.

"Don't worry," the sedationist says, her voice warm and firm. "This will help you be more productive later and won't take long."

"Well, all right then," you relent, concluding that the best way to get rid of the sedationist is to go along with her.

You swivel your task chair around to face us, to get this over with. "Great. First, let's sit down on the sofa," she instructs.

She takes the lead and with gracefully sweeping strides moves past you to the small sofa facing the window. You follow and sit down beside her.

"Now, I'd like you to drink this. Slowly."

After unscrewing the cap from it, she hands you the thermos. You take it and bring its mouth to yours. She watches you intently, as if her gaze will grab you should you guzzle down the contents too quickly. You take one gulp. There's a long pause before you raise the thermos to your lips again. Not because you're following her instructions to drink slowly, but because you're preoccupied.

"Take your time," she encourages with a small smile.

Then, with each mouthful you take from the thermos, you appear to become more and more detached from the work you were so obsessed with. It's as if the milk were loosening your mind's grip, its fixation upon the tasks you felt were so dire.

When you've finished everything in the thermos, you hand it back to the sedationist, who places it lightly on the walnut flooring.

"Now, tell me about one of the places you felt most comfortable in, when you were a child," she tells you.

"Oh, my favorite is my grandparents' house," you reply, nostalgia tinging your heart. "It was the kind of place where you could just let time pass, and it would all be okay. Like everything was in its place. Not that things were meticulously organized, but they were where they should be. Where they made sense to be in a home."

The sedationist nods and murmurs the occasional, "Mmhmm," assuringly.

As you continue describing the atmosphere of the apartment, it all feels so vivid to me. I remember the place so well. The sounds and smells of urban bustle coming in through open windows, the outside world hectic but the inner one created there serene.

As your voice grows softer, the sedationist does something so gradually, fluidly and naturally that I almost don't notice it, but when I do, it surprises me. Having somehow placed her right arm around your right shoulder, she slowly draws you towards her until you are leaning against her. She strokes your arm lightly. Your eyelids begin to droop.

"Thanks, that really did the trick," I tell her as we have tea at the kitchen table.

"Well, this will do for the short term," she tells me. "But if the underlying issues go unaddressed, it's only a matter of time before this kind of workaholic freak out strikes again."

"What should we do?" I ask.

The cat rubs his head against my leg. I reach down to stroke him.

"Seems like this is the result of contingent worth spiraling out of control, because it isn't counterbalanced with intrinsic value," she explains. "So a confidence-building workshop or attachment-strengthening exercises should be effective."

"Strange. Characteristics like confidence have been robust before."

"Then they may have gotten rattled or overlooked. Mindfulness training should stabilize them. Hypnotherapy or appreciation exercises could also resolve this."

"Okay, I'll look into that. Thanks."

"I can recommend someone, if you'd like," she says before finishing her tea. "Just let me know."

But the bill from the sedationist doesn't leave much, if anything for another intervention. I wonder for a moment if this is calling your sense of worth into question. Low financial net worth can really overshadow one's positive qualities. But even if that is the root cause, there's very little I can do to improve your cash flow. And that leads me to realize that I can either *(a)* identify and remove whatever is diminishing your perception of your value or *(b)* I can increase your awareness of your qualities. The latter seems much easier. The former will be time intensive, involving the analysis of various arenas of your life, finding the issues and troubleshooting them with you. Even if time weren't an issue, I'm not sure I have what it takes to pull this off.

To avoid another frenzied pseudo-productivity binge, I decide to give hypnosis a shot. We dabbled in the power of suggestion some years ago, when you thought I might be able to use it to change your habits and also induce lucid dreaming. I still remember the techniques you had us learn. Counting the steps while descending the spiral staircase into the subconscious. Imagining ethereal projection out a window and into the landscape beyond. Deep breathing connected to the expansion of the body concept to include the trees near us.

In the evening, when you're once again spacing out with your tea, when it will be easy to lull you into a more suggestive state, I seize the opportunity.

"Your arms and legs feel really heavy," I whisper assertively to you. "Like fatigue is spewing gravitons from them."

"Yeah, really," you murmur.

"Close your eyes to rest them. Imagine now the scenery of that hike we took a few weeks ago. The mountainous expanse. The smell of roseberry."

You give no response, not even a slight nod. That's exactly what I want.

"Virstea Peak is your confidence. The emerald lake at its base is my love for you. The sky is your creativity. Trindeol Forest is your hope," I instruct you.

Since each of these is a constant facet of the landscape, they will let you know that the qualities important to you are always there and are robust. Ugly incidents at work and financial woes, those won't impact these features of the landscape and therefore won't impact your confidence, your creativity and my love.

I repeat these correspondences between your life and the landscape, until I've said the words enough times to feel like they state a new reality. Then I just watch you breathe, reassured by this steady rhythm.

For the next week, you are calm and collected, in high spirits. You can focus meaningfully on work and make progress that matters.

But soon, you're spending more and more time in Conolo Valley. It starts with a half-hour cloud-gazing session, followed by an hour-long hike the next day, then an afternoon of picnicking and sunbathing the day after. At first, I'm delighted that you're at last making time to be outdoors, to be away from work and amid nature. But soon, you're bicycling over every chance you get, staying there for hours on end. Walking many of the wending trails, sitting contentedly on the grassy hillside like you exist outside the flow of time, sketching the landscape in your notebook engrossed to the point of filling page after page with pencil lines and charcoal shading.

Concerned by this new and intensifying habit, I ask you what's going on.

"It just feels so great to be there," you answer. "Somehow, I feel reassured. I feel more me there than anywhere else I've been recently. It's starting to feel weird not being there."

You think for a moment, then add, "I love staring at Virstea and hearing the burble of Toringul Creek. The skies are so bright, and the clouds are gorgeous."

Of course. I should have known. You want to feel in touch with your confidence and hope. Feel secure and in tune with your inner cosmos by way of its outer correlates. You want to be unequivocally immersed in the validation they provide. Who wouldn't want that?

It seems obviously inevitable now that my amateur hypno-therapy would result in this. If only the answer to this complica-tion were just as obvious.

I spend days on end brainstorming up possible solutions, but each comes up short. I consider changing the associations so that trees nearby are connected to your confidence, but then you'd just end up spending chunks of your day staring at or climbing into them. I could link your confidence to the strawberry jam in the fridge, but rather than leaving that safely in the refrigerator, you might carry the jar around to take frequent breaks to eat jam on scones, toast, yogurt, crackers, then panic when the jar was empty. If confidence is just in the air you breathe, will you just be content spending your time inhaling deeply, exhaling slowly, feeling it enter and circulate through your body? What about in-stilling confidence in the ring Mom gave you? Would you fidget with the ring incessantly, rubbing at it with a fingertip to feel the solidity of confidence encircling your finger?

But while I'm getting lost in myriad plans and their contin-gencies, you find your own answer.

I don't notice it at first, but you come home later and lat-er in the evenings, presumably spending more time at work. At first, I think you've been assigned a new project or are scrambling to make up for the time you've spent out in Conolo. But then I notice that your mood outside of work is increasingly one of thoughtful distraction, of contemplative daydreaming. Work never puts you in this state of mind. There must be something different—new—going on. Something captivating enough to keep you from Conolo Valley.

And when you come home this evening with a big, goofy grin, I know it definitely can't be work.

"So what's the big secret?" I ask.

This snaps you out of your euphoria.

"Oh," you murmur sheepishly. "Well, I was planning to just show you, but we won't have a working version for another couple days."

"We?"

"Yeah, a group of us at work. Qalixy had an intriguing idea for a qualia-altering device, and we'd gather at lunch and coffee time or spontaneously in the hallways to talk about it. Then last week, Zusern volunteered his basement as a workspace. So we've been working on getting this technology to work. It's called the *The Awegmenter*, and it amplifies the qualities of objects so they feel amazing. It can also do the opposite. There's a commonplacer setting that dials down how extraordinary something is. Essentially quotidifies objects and events."

"So basically *The Awegmenter* makes things seem more or less amazing?"

"Yes, it works with the idea of awedinariness, that in the ordinary lies the awesome and vice versa. That relationship just needs to be emphasized."

"Hmm," I murmur as I muse upon how this technology could boost our appreciation of the quotidian.

"I was thinking we could use the prototype next week to have the most understated grilled cheese sandwich and also stand by the most wondrous aspen tree."

The excitement in your voice is thick and languid.

To eat a grilled cheese sandwich as if it's just one of millions like it, as just heated dairy protein and fat on crisped carbs. To see an aspen like it's the only one or last of its kind, or as a singular achievement of nature. To behold a sunset as merely another sunset and then as the only sunset of that day. To know a kiss as a fleeting, wondrous bodily expression of ethereal emotions, then know it as but one instance of a romantic ideal enacted over and over throughout human history.

You seek now to be an artist of experience, molding the materials of perception into visceral significance—or insignificance. To shape consciousness at this level is to grapple with the very essence of meaning in being human. Is confidence prerequisite to that, becoming simply the backdrop to the stage of enactment? Or have you now gained another source of confidence?

Regardless, you are bringing us further into the territory of taking each other for granted as a means of being special to one another. I place a hand on your shoulder, ready for this journey.

As Night Fades

To be honest, if you hadn't described its languorous glombozling to me, I would have misinterpreted the brext's blurry clombulating form as something else—a womberlaft practicing courtship displays, maybe. Or I could have missed it entirely.

I don't tell you any of that, but I'm sure you sense it.

This fits into the pattern that has been building up: I am less and less the one to excitedly point out some facet of the nocturnal world that surrounds us—that role is now nearly completely filled by you. Like birding with aunt Janine: she's always the one to spot the birds, telling me where to aim my binoculars.

And you know as well as I do that the situation is very evidently, very rapidly getting worse. What was a nagging suspicion has become an undeniable, intrusive certainty. My once sharp views of nocturnal beings and happenings have been steadily growing fuzzy and faint. There is no rationalizing it away now. My night vision is deteriorating. As we knew one day it would.

Soon, darkness will appear emptier to me, no longer populated by the creatures and mysterious objects and strange, shadowy possibilities that I once saw so vividly, now blearily. Then the quiet gloom of night will feel much calmer and much lonelier.

"Over there to the left," you say to me, voice hushed as usual. "See that fluttering? Looks like the hunting's good tonight."

My eyes move to what your words are pointing out. And I see her. Though brush obscures some of her frolic, the fluid complexity of her swiftly undulating tendrils is unmistakably indicative of a successful episode of foraging. She has returned invigorated to actively cogitate.

"Oh, nice," I whisper back. "She's seems more demonstrative since I saw her a couple weeks ago."

"She's been by the lake recently. Maybe she's happy to be back here."

Hearing that is a relief to me. Finding out she's been here all along and I haven't noticed, that would have been heartbreaking. More heartbreaking than her impending invisibility to me already is.

I will miss this wernackle, her feathery nighttime camouflage perfect for perching atop trees and drifting through the skies, her graceful fluidity of kinesthetic thinking. But what I will really miss, of course, is you.

If seeing reality more clearly means not seeing you at all, then I don't want it. I don't want the adult ability of tightly focusing the mind's eye, I don't want that unavoidable mode of perception to erase the world I share with you. Seeing plausibilities in sharp detail in broad daylight can't possibly compare to this.

"Do you think I will still be able to hear your voice?" I asked you last week.

"If I still sound clear to you now, then probably," you answered.

Now so accustomed to seeing you—that familiar silhouette seated in my room, standing in the backyard against the dark woods, walking beside me in those woods—I couldn't imagine what it would be like once you became invisible but remained audible.

So I asked, "How will I know you're here?"

"I'll tell you. Or I'll whistle or hum," you answered, unfazed. That was reassuring.

I don't ask such questions now. They are too sad, and there's too much to enjoy with you here, even with the waning clarity.

So we watch the visitors from other realms—the ustilam, clorftas and many more—as they cross the skies, here to admire, study or just pass through our world. They take a multitude of forms as dense flocks, lines and streamers, loose sheets and bulbous billows. Tonight, some Norlarians ride together upon vaporous vehicles, each like a cross between a cloud and a bus then crossed with a flying carpet. Beneath them, like ever swirling grids of points, inspection crews meticulously scour for inconsistencies, anything out of place that the next wave of maintenance crews should smooth away or excise. They do their job expertly, combing entire swaths of the world before dawn to make sure everything is in order for the daytime. You told me that once you saw a tiny patch of sky by the horizon still glowing with twilight. It was beautiful, but before midnight, they had darkened it out.

Abruptly, a small bulging of sky gets my attention.

"Do you see that?" I blurt, hand flinging upward.

As it points to the distant glomming sphere, my fingertip is just barely visible against the swath of sky between the mountain peaks.

"Is that a time displacement bubble?" you ask.

"Yes, it's got to be a future archaeologist!"

I'm thrilled I can still make out the anachronistic bead. From here, it's lentil-sized, but it must be the size of a hot air balloon.

"Wow. I always forget how they so smoothly deform the world," you remark. "Like a stray, prescient thought tactfully poking the fabric of the mind."

"There's really nothing like it," I murmur.

We watch it for a while. I wonder who is on the other side watching our world, how does that future see its past. Is it at all like if I were to observe myself as a baby, or like seeing my grandmother now?

Then, my eyes wander to a faint, wafting plume from behind Denslir Peak. Someone over there is letting go of their secrets, letting them dissipate into the night. The clorftas dart through it like it's not there at all, but this vaporous ascension is countless secrets, maybe a lifetime of them, rarefied now so that nothing can hold on to them. Was this transformation the result of conscious choice, or fatigue, or eventual indifference?

"It's getting late," my mother calls from down the path.

You place a claw lightly on my shoulder and tell me, "See you tomorrow."

I wish I could say the same thing.

I reply, "I'll be here," instead, matching the certainty in your voice.

Agents of Socially Distributed Cognition

1

I press it upon her warm, open, outstretched palm. The exchange makes me keenly aware that this will likely be the last time I see this nugget of validation that I've been holding on to for about a week and a half now, until we could both make the trip to this observatory atop Kaleidoscope Mountain to meet in person.

To preempt her appraisal of this compact bundle of peer affirmation as meager, I'm tempted to say, "There's plenty more where that came from." I want to tell her that I've put some aside, stored a sizable portion to age and acquire nuance. But I'm afraid that then she'll want and be impatient for more, that she won't treat what she holds now as valuable.

A chill creeps into me. I lean back in my chair and zip up my jacket, as if to prevent the mountainous, elemental landscape outside the window behind her from pulling the warmth from my body.

The longer she remains silent, the more I want to also tell her that being the custodian of her validation has kept me vitalized. Contact with this form of existential acknowledgement keeps me buoyant, and without it, I could do little more than doggy paddle in the viscous tedium of urban life. And to know that she can regularly elicit from people one of the vital materials of esteem—

ultimately of self-worth—and to know that people can effortlessly furnish this genuine substance, being privy to such knowledge quietly amazes and heartens me. Because people can be stingy, highly selective when it comes to offering appreciation, convinced that few are deserving, leaving many impoverished of it.

Her reticence makes the air feel disconcertingly still, and I have to remind myself that what can seem like disappointment or nonchalance is likely consideration. Her mind needs time to sample the texture of this condensed social feedback, to fathom the layered depth of the acceptance comprising it.

I distract myself by looking at the loose cluster of meerkat owls standing outside. They have convened upon a patch of bare, fractured granite, assembled into another social yet solitary gathering of these lankiest of all owls in which they acknowledge each other's presence silently with the affordance of space. Their eyes are wide and very lemony yellow. Rendered in afternoon sunlight unabated by clouds, the world right now must seem very bright to them.

Suddenly yet gracefully, one owl takes flight, swiftly and majestically unfurling and flapping its impossibly grand, rusty wings. I want to point out this splendid event to her. She, like the remaining owls, seems oblivious or impervious to this awesome departure. The demeanor of the owls strikes me as almost meditative now, as though they are collectively engaged in individual mindfulness. Perhaps they are each consolidating their memories, firming up what has been cognitively distilled from past experiences.

"Thank you," she says warmly, bringing my attention back inside, back to her.

"My pleasure," I reply, because it is. My work for her is enjoyable. You made sure I got through all the unpleasant work—all the work that had to be unpleasant because I was new to everything you had long since mastered.

She reaches into her coat pocket and removes a twine-bound packet of images.

"I thought you might enjoy these," she says, holding out the bundle over the small table between our chairs.

"Oh, how nice of you," I reply, taking the images.

"I'd like you to take something back with you, besides memories, after coming all this way."

I nod, smiling.

"Can you recommend a good massage place?" she asks.

Though oddly timed, her words are fluid and amiable and remind me that we're still new at this. The relationship isn't natural for either of us. Yet.

"Sure," I answer and describe several to her.

Moments like this during our meetings encourage me to wonder what our interactions would be like if we didn't have this arrangement. I like to think we'd be listening to a gently cerebral jazz quartet, talking about humanity's evolutionary heritage, in the evening hours when it's all too easy to become curious and anxious about the fundamentals of who we are.

2

While making my way down the mountain's east-face hiking trail, which is intermittently full of scree and corrugated with tree roots, I rest by a stream that must be crossed with an arcing sequence of jagged stepping stones. I drink from the water bottle I usually carry on trips like this, then look at a couple of the visual representations she's given me. For a good while, I stare at the one of the girl on a patio stretching her senses. I hold it up in front of me, against a backdrop of tall cedars, as if to contextualize or contrast it with my surroundings.

The extension of her hearing is well rendered, but what remote portions of the soundscape she is reaching toward, that is not depicted. What little noises that would otherwise slip by, what faint sounds is she able to touch? Is she catching the scratching of butter knives on toast? Is the light rippling of meadow grass brushing her expanded auditory awareness?

With quiet wistfulness, the scene reminds me of the piano sonata "Winterless Months." Both capture the feeling of reaching for the quotidian yet ethereal, nostalgic and ultimately elusive. Seeking what is beyond our grasp because to touch it fleetingly would be enough.

3

I don't see her again for several weeks. During which I accrue more validation for her, sporadically through the usual channels: meetings, mail and artwork. It's mostly mail during this time, little parcels of articulated appreciation sent to my office. After reviewing them, after feeling their delightful, intriguing and nuanced textures, I enter their particulars in the logs; their date of arrival, origins, extent, intensity and composition are all recorded along with a simple sketch. With the documentation complete, I put them in the distillation apparatus one at a time, tune the purification parameters, and let the essence concentrate into a series of small bottles. The consistency and vividity of the refinement output are then noted in the logs. When there's enough for the next step, I swiftly but carefully combine and mold the distillates into a cohesive form, just as you taught me. You'd be pleased by how smoothly this work now proceeds.

Only two meetings punctuate my handling of this mail, the first with a young syntactician and the other with a curiosity consultant. Both are brief.

"There's something... unobviously but unmistakably transfigurational about her comments," says the syntactician, leaning forward on the picnic table. "There's a certain magic in conversing with her."

I find this curious. Apparently she often evokes that feeling in others too. It's a prevalent motif in the esteem I receive for her. Yet I've never experienced anything like it in our meetings, but perhaps this magic awaits us in our future conversations on Kaleidoscope Mountain.

Of course, I don't say anything about my thoughts or otherwise. I simply raise my eyebrows and nod, encouraging him to continue, to add more into the open jar on the wooden planks of the table, just to my left.

"There's a sheer, incredulous, quiet joy of being in those moments with her, of knowing that such a moment is possible."

His voice is like fog billowing slowly toward me, floating through the air. Behind him sway the withering stems of wildflowers in the prairie. The world is hypnotizing me, to make me receptive to its suggestion that I need not search elsewhere for the ethereal.

"It allows me to find that kind of joy in other moments, like this one now," he adds. "That's in part what I mean by magic."

That's the magic of being human, I want to tell him.

The muscles of my face take on a subdued glow, and it takes me a moment to realize that this is the doing not of the sun's warmth on my cheeks but of a subtle smile. I will have to make note of this when I catalog this conversation.

4

The rest of—really the majority of—my time in the office is spent in its messy regions examining episodic memories placed in my care, then synthesizing the artificial ones required to fill the gaps among them.

That process is nearly complete for my most eccentric client yet, R75a. One of her hobbies is building a mental collection of colorful numbers that she encounters in signage, product packaging, artwork and miscellaneous other places; with these, she constructs a spectrum for each digit. Recently, R75a has found several numerals are missing a few of their chromatic variants. The bluest number 5, especially, has been forgotten. My task has been to re-complete her spectra for 2, 5 and 8 as well as re-create the soothing-green 3 and spicy-orange 9.

It has been painstaking work to interpolate the proper hues from memory residues and cross-correlating them with her color qualia, aesthetic sensibilities and emotional associations, but with that at last done, all that's left for this assignment is to perform the final check on the imaginatively constructed fakes for inconsistencies, then integrate the fabricated core memories and their peripherals with her existing memories. That takes only a few afternoons of episodic work, after which I turn everything over to my reviewer for verification.

The subsequent project concerns the concoction of postcards and their messages for VI76a, an early-career voice instructor. All throughout his well-traveled childhood (of precocious cosmopolitanism developed by his father's career as a curiosity consultant), VI76a's mother would frequently urge him to make the most of the age of extensive postal connectivity that she said they were fortunate to inhabit. She insisted that he always carry postcards or letter-writing stationary and have the addresses of friends on hand—or better yet, memorized. Idle moments on a bus or waiting for the dentist, she suggested, could be spent composing a brief greeting or life update on a postcard, to be later sent off via a nearby mailbox to some distant friend.

She essentially wanted him to harness postal connectivity to maintain and strengthen social connectivity. So in his youth, VI76a became a prolific postcard writer but has since forgotten much of what he wrote during the post-college period spent fulfilling his wanderlust. I've been hired by VI76a to obscure that fact from his future selves because he identifies that time of his life as seminal to his "crystallization of character."

This is one of my more challenging assignments, as it involves places I have not visited, cultures I have not encountered let alone been immersed in. I have to devote greater attention to the details in VI76a's extant memories and photographs of his travels. In addition to gathering the elements of his memories with the most salience, I pluck out minutiae and miscellaneous musings that would fit the kind of correspondences he had with his friends.

Sometimes it's easy. Bits of memories are tinged, even ear-marked with associations to friends. The Trunderblufan custom of regularly buying fresh flowers for home decoration caught his attention only because it brought to mind Hinoko, who was a flower aficionado. With a group of tourists also riding the train to Cerfa, he made small talk with phrases learned years ago from his exchange student roommate Zoflé. These are the kinds of moments that I re-engineer in his memories into the basis of the postcard messages. Most of the time, I have to be inventive about the impetus for—the backstory to—the postcard writing.

Fortunately, my work is aided by two key characteristics of this client: VI76a's writing style is casual and nondescript, and his selection of postcards is driven largely by images that pertain to his travel experiences, particularly those that relate to the interests of the intended recipient. This makes the forgery of postcards and their messages thankfully straightforward. And the fact of the matter is that though this era of his life may have been the crucible from which his current identity was cast, it has played its role, and even if the postcards he wrote then were of critical significance, his memory of them is not. Their forgettable nature suggests that their messages were not tremendously valuable or unique. No hints of what was on those postcards linger in his intact memories, suggesting that he didn't pay much attention to them. Attention is the foundation of most memories, and without attention, without thoughtfulness, it is unlikely the postcard messages he did author were as significant as VI76a is convinced they are.

Inevitably, as I go about all this forging of faux memories, I recall what you said about it.

"Once your validation work has a good track record, when it's earned you the recognition to secure a couple distinguished wards, you won't have to confabulate anymore."

While you regarded the trade of memory filling as a respectable profession, proficiency in validation keeping was incomparably more admirable. An insubvertibly worthwhile way to sustain one's self financially, socially and psychologically.

I do prefer focusing my efforts on validation, but I don't know if I'd be able to do it all the time. There's something mundanely mesmerizing in the construction of memories for others. For now.

"Validation is the key to manifesting one of the psyche's truest essences," you'd say. "That's what you can make possible. It may only happen just a handful of times, or it could be routine. But it's bound to happen at least once. And when it does, so many other emotional and cognitive transactions will become paltry to you."

I'm afraid that one day I'll find out you're right. That everything else will become trite in comparison. That I'll become obsessed with validation keeping as a means to an end.

5

Just when I start to worry about her, a brief letter arrives. In it, she gives her regards and suggests a few meeting dates.

I'm startled by the magnitude of relief her simple message gives me. The letter dissolves an emotional load I didn't know I had been carrying. I entertain the thought of the timing as deliberate, as if she knew how long it would take for me to become concerned and sought to mitigate the growing unease. That's farfetched but could contain a kernel of truth, that she contacted me to allay any apprehensions she thought I might have. But of course, I have no idea what her motivations really are.

When she convenes these meetings, I never know if it's because she's in need of validation or if it's finally convenient for her to make the trip to the observatory. You've always told me these kinds of things don't matter. The validation keeper's responsibility is only to collect and hand over esteem in an amount and form that's appropriate.

6

We meet under a sky that looks like a permuting patchwork of pastel hues. With the ever colder weather, the atmospheric fluctuations visible at the summit of Kaleidoscope Mountain become much more pronounced, rapidly altering the ambient chromaticity. It's as if the mountain must earn its name again every year with this annual accentuation of the mini-aurora above it.

When she steps off one of the lift cars, I'm there waiting for her on the platform of the upper gondola station. As she walks toward me, across the wooden planks of the platform, we exchange smiles. The breezy air all around us smells faintly of anise.

In the observatory's viewing parlor, she tells me that the massage was very relaxing and that these recent weeks have passed by quickly with curiosity and exploration.

"Not exactly eventful but engrossing," she encapsulates.

"Were they wondrous but not wonderful?" I conjecture.

"Yes," she answers brightly, as if with tacit laughter.

"It's good to hear you've been well."

"Thank you. You seem well too."

"It's been the usual, which is good," I tell her.

She nods understandingly, then looks into my eyes for a moment that becomes quite long. I remove the nugget of validation from my jacket pocket. A moment later, it's rolling from my hand into hers.

She closes her eyes and takes a deep breath.

"It's very nicely condensed," she says, opening her eyes.

"I was given some excellent sentiments to work with."

She blinks slowly, thoughtfully, reminding me that winter is approaching. I glance at her watch, long enough to know that it's stopped. I'm about to mention this to her, but there's a feeling of familiarity to the erroneous time displayed on the watch face. Perhaps the hands were already immobile the last time we were here, and I become aware that she does not wear this watch to keep the current time.

"I'll be traveling for a while," she tells me.

Before I can ask where, she adds, "I'm not sure when I'll be back, but I'll be in touch with letters."

And immediately I'm seized by the impulse to offer her more validation, give her the extra you've told me always to bring to these meetings, just in case.

This urge orients my attention to her demeanor. There's a resolute poise to her presence. She doesn't need the validation I've just given her. She is headed off for travel because she has plenty of validation, enough to propel her to venture away from here.

"Will you be visiting places where your watch will run?" I wonder, accidentally aloud.

As if by reflex her right hand jerks over her watch. I take the sudden motion of her hand as admonition, like it could have been a swift slap in the face; my psyche shrinks back, and I regret allowing my curiosity to reveal itself so spontaneously.

Slowly her palm then fingers recede from her left wrist, finally leaving the inert timepiece exposed again.

"Yes, I hope so," she says. "I'll tell you more about my watch the next time I see you. For now, I'll tell you what was happening the moment I stopped it, if you'd like."

I nod.

"Have you been to Nolinga Canyon?" she asks.

"No, I haven't heard of it before."

"If you have a chance to spend some time there, it's well worthwhile. There are questions embedded throughout the landscape that you'll find as you make your way through it. I was there several years ago with my parents and younger brother. The morning of our last full day there, I was hiking one of the ridge trails with them, when one of those questions appeared right before me. *What here has your future favorite colors?*

"It was like the world was prodding me to consider, just a little bit, who I was going to become. Then an amethyst bunting darted by, and I just instantly pulled at the crown of my watch. That barely conscious action may have been just nonsensical fiddling at the time, but I ended up infusing it with a significance I culled from my ruminations and introspection over the next couple of days. That's what I'll tell you about when we meet again. Or perhaps in the letters I send you."

"Okay."

This briefest of verbal acknowledgements seems all that I can reciprocate in exchange for this installment of explanation.

In the following silence, our eyes are drawn to the prismatic sky. Watching the amalgam of pulsating and wavering hues, it occurs to me that we should perhaps be eating pickles and chips as spectators of this swath of sky.

"Do you ever think about who else's validation you could be managing?" she asks.

"Only very occasionally now. For a short time after we had completed our training, members of my cohort would get together to hang out. Some would talk at length about who they had been matched with. When you hear about the details, you can't help but imagine how you'd feel in those situations they described."

"What did you tell them about me?"

"Only that I couldn't tell if you looked forward at all to receiving validation. Whether the validation was what you expected."

"Oh?"

"Quorina said her ward was always nervous, because he was afraid of the possibility of getting little or no validation. Or that it would be highly conditional or tentative. She thought that you might be similar, that perhaps you were uncertain. I told her our situation was different. You seemed glad to see me but indifferent or reserved toward the validation."

"Well, those are both generally somewhat true. Meeting with you is a refreshing change of pace. And you know what to do when it comes to validation. I know I can leave it to you and not worry."

You would be delighted to hear this.

"Thanks. I had a skilled and supportive mentor," I reply.

"I wish I had had someone like that," she says with a very matter-of-fact tone.

*But you will **be** someone like that, and that's even better*, I want to tell her. Of this I'm certain, from all the validation I've concentrated and given to her. But that's not for me to say. That will or has already come through the work I do for her.

"Good mentors are easier to come by in some fields than others," is all I can offer trivially instead.

"Culture has been my mentor in the absence of others."

"Isn't she a tough one? To decipher and rely on?"

"Yes, you must be selective which lessons to take from her. She requires you be an attentive and discerning apprentice."

Her words make me all the more thankful for your unequivocal guidance.

"And so you're off to learn from her again," I surmise.

"Inevitably, but I had a different teacher in mind this time."

The warm firmness of her voice suggests to me that she intends to learn from nature, curiosity, family or herself—something immediate, focalized yet boundless, made deeply ambient by the human mind.

I nod, acknowledging the importance of having a particular instructor selected or kept in mind. That's of course a vital part of knowing how to learn; knowing who to learn from.

"Can I ask you," she says, "what is it that you do besides... handle my validation?"

"I'm a confabulist," I answer automatically, as I have count-less times before.

Her eyes widen. She must never have guessed this was my primary occupation.

"You're a memory maker?" she paraphrases to mentally pro-cess this facet of my identity.

I nod.

After a moment, she says, "Do you, um... okay, I guess you can't tell me any more."

"Oh, I know what you're thinking. Don't worry, all the work I do is directly with clients for their own personal needs."

Her eyebrows and forehead crease with confusion.

"Clients?" she echoes in inquiry. "But who would *want* confabulations?"

"Well, it bothers some people when they can't remember certain things. So they'd rather have their memory seem intact, even if it's made whole with fictitious information. Like say back in third grade you had a really good friend, and now you can't remember what you used to talk so excitedly about together. Maybe that really bothers you, because it's upsetting that you *know* you had such fantastic times with this friend, yet you can't recall what particularly was so fantastic, and you can't ask this friend because you have no way to get in contact. To fill this gap in your memory, you'd give me what you do remember, along with other memories you have of this friend, your childhood habits and any other memories that might be relevant for fab-ricating convincing replacements or fillers or however you want to think about it. That's a simplistic example but sums up the essentials of the process."

After a moment of consideration, she says, "That all make sense. But what about the friend? Even if the memories you make for me are self-consistent with my own memories, the confabula-tion is likely to be inconsistent with this friend's memories."

I smile and reflect that I should have known she wouldn't have been satisfied with the oversimplified description of my work.

"Okay, yes, that's where it gets philosophical," I answer. "If you never see this third-grade friend again, does it matter? And say this friend does re-enter your life, and the two of you talk about those great third grade days you had together. Two things could happen. The friend doesn't clearly remember that time and accepts the confabulations you recount. In which case, you both now have in your memories a fictional interpolation of your shared past. Is that better than both of you having only vague recollections of that past? Perhaps. The other scenario is that the friend disputes your account of the third grade friendship, and the discrepancy needs to be resolved, likely by some discussion that will result in the editing of your memories or your friend's memories or both. That might eliminate one set of memories entirely or synthesize them together into a consistent narrative. But again, does it matter? Does the obliteration of accurate recollections or its hybridization with a fiction have any appreciable impact on your life? That can be highly subjective."

"So there's a risk of your work turning the past contentious," she muses. "But I suppose it already is when it comes to our memories."

"Exactly. On some level, the past is over, and our memories are just stories about it. Does it matter if those stories differ from a previous state of reality? Well, yes and no. How we think about the past impacts how we act in the present and plan for the future. But the world is the way it is regardless of how we view the past. Which matters more to you, or how do you balance those perspectives? That could be the central question here."

"But that's a question that may never come up for some of your clients. Hopefully most of them," she surmises.

"Yes. So before all that, it's a question of how likely inconsistencies are to arise and how much impact disruption they could cause. Clients come to me knowing the answer already, even if only on an unconscious level."

"And your clients are fine having these false memories because they won't know they're counterfeit and they're ready to live with the possible consequences?"

"Yes, if I've done a good job, the forgery is indistinguishable from other memories and has little chance of being problematic. I remove their memories of missing memories, so they won't remember what specifically they've forgotten. They'll remember using my services, but they won't know what for."

"Wow. You must be quite the memory artist."

"The key is to put only enough detail so that the mind in remembering can fill in the rest. Much of what we call memory relies on imagination. A different kind of focused creativity, but it is imagination nonetheless. We all are quite the memory artists."

She grins at this unveiling of commonplace genius, at this crucial yet mundane, domestic necessity of imagination.

"Thanks for telling me about all this," she says, words full of a sort of significance.

"Glad to. I get to find out all kinds of things about you all the time, so it's nice to reciprocate."

"Tell me more after I get back," she says brightly.

"Sure," I answer.

"I'll be looking forward to that."

She rises from her seat, bringing our meeting to its conclusion.

"Let me know if I should mail you some validation," I offer, just in case.

"I will," she assures me.

"Safe travels," I wish her.

"Thank you, and be well," she replies.

7

In the following weeks I take on two new confabulation projects, while continuing to fabricate an assortment of past correspondences for VI76a. When I work on that for long stretches of time, I feel like a prolific, unrequited pen pal with the past or with an alternate history.

About a tenth of my actual, current mail tells me she is still traveling and in good spirits. Her latest postcard features a stunning close-up of a marigold zephyr with wings outspread as it skims the surface of a lake porcelain green with glacial waters. On the other side of the postcard are two short paragraphs. The first describes the alpine landscape she's been hiking through. The second merely states that her watch has been running for several days now and with the correct time, its ticking sometimes soothing, other times unnerving.

That comment makes me wonder if she has forgotten how relentless time is.

Much of the remaining mail tells me that she still has an appreciable presence here. Everything sent to me by her friends and colleagues reveals that the crucial essence of her personality resonates in their lives: that magic of thoughtful listening, genuine curiosity, sincere concern and acute observancy. Admiration, reassurance, communion, respect, affection, I refine them all for her, reminded of all that I once felt and now feel for you.

Sometimes, if I'm tired, it's easy to mistake that interplay of my memories and the appreciation others have for her as the reason why I do this work. But it is simply the flowering of an already magnificently growing tree. The memory of which will be enough to sustain me when this tree is bare in the depths of winter. To you, the ephemerality of these blossoms would be itself complete—the memory, what we mentally preserve of the experience, just extra. But I'm not there yet.

Dynamics of Dislocation

It's been a couple of weeks now, and you haven't snapped out of it. Emotionally, you're still stagnant and distant. Your thoughts cover new ground, but your heart has remained stuck. Like it's been left behind by your mind, by time itself and therefore us, and is now resigned to be mired in insecurity and a longing for humanity's lost grandeur, while everything else moves ever onward to new, fresh emotions. What started as a change in mood has once again gone on to become a change in personality. So it's time to go on the trip I've promised to take, to make the pickup.

When I unfold the handwritten directions that have been waiting for this day, I'm mentally transported back to that morning you made your request as we brunched at a small table in the Relupho delicatessen.

"If I'm in one of *those* emotional phases again, I need you to go to this address as soon as you can and tell the receptionist who you are," you instructed several months ago, over plates of kakiage, apple fritters, pickled garlic and takenoko gohan. "The rest will be explained to you there."

"All right," I agreed, trusting you because I knew I could and because these "phases" were becoming a drain on your social life and work.

"Thanks," you said after receiving this agreement you never doubted I'd give you.

"Glad to help," I said to you for the first time in a while.

Along with the address, you gave me some simplistic directions and basic instructions, then made no further mention of the matter.

Even if it was vague and secretive, I was encouraged to know that you had a plan for the "phases" when they returned. Something must be done. They render you only half present, allowing you to be intellectually active while keeping you emotionally sluggish, displaced from us. At festive gatherings like Zona's speculative dinner parties, the delight of convivial company comes to you tardy and muted. When the hotly anticipated discovery of inter-relational deep causal structure was announced, your mind grasped the consequential significance of this, but the poignancy never fully dawned upon you. You had been denied emotional connection to the fundamental physical workings of our world. The latest research conclusively demonstrated that every present moment has all possible pasts but that we could never know any of them but the one in our memories. And we knew then we are just a chapter to which all possible preludes had been written. It was disconcerting to see that one of the most landmark discoveries of our lifetime elicited so little emotion from you.

That still bothers me. Each moment of our lives, the decisions we make, everything we do doesn't only winnow future possibilities but also spawns alternate pasts. That fills me with a keen loneliness. It's like trailing behind us are now all the worlds we could have come from. Like we're ever creating and elaborating our ancestry. But we will never know that expanding pedigree. And only much later were you able to feel the impact of this paradigm shift. Its initial emotional tidal wave lifted all of us while you were submerged in your emotional scuba dive. You could only feel the elevation of its subsiding swell when you surfaced.

I follow your directions, like they're a treasure map on weathered parchment. They take me down country roads, canyon trails, through urban forests and finally into cobblestone alleyways—paths that I have never taken through our neighboring cities. As I make my way to the address you've given me, I think occasionally of that scientific breakthrough. I become eerily aware that every step I take places me in a present that has multiple pasts unknown to me. But how many possible ways are there to make this journey with the directions you've given me and with the quasi-deterministic nature of our universe?

However many there are, they all end up bringing me to an ancient apartment building now recessed into an overcrowded fashion district. Before entering, I consider the tetrachromatic, aspirational posters on the walls, then the drafting tables I can see through the windows, and finally the bronzed gadgets heaped decoratively by the doorway and prominent signs for the loading dock. It seems to be some kind of obscure design consultancy.

When I step into the small lobby, the world seems to rarefy, become reduced in its density of people, objects and events. There's barely anything here but a receptionist, her desk, cushy armchairs and plain walls, lots of walls joining or running past each other at a variety of angles. There's even a stark quality to the receptionist, who has just enough warmth to be quintessentially human and feminine.

I walk over to the receptionist's desk, and as you instructed, I give my name. She doesn't smile exactly but acknowledges my introduction with a flattening of her lips together and slight brightening of her eyes. The subtle expression is reminiscent of the early stages of smile, what precedes that which we typically recognize as a smile. A proto-smile.

"Please have a seat," the receptionist says.

As I sit down in one of the armchairs by the window, I hear her say, "We have a pickup for project HJ," presumably into an intercom system.

My eyes defocus on the butter-yellow wall several feet in front of me. If I had a can of paint with me, preferably mediocre orange, I'd splash it on that wall and watch it dribble down.

A couple minutes later, a woman wearing an ocean blue sweater and beige corduroy cargo pants walks over to me.

"Hello," she greets me.

I rise from the chair to shake her hand, which is soft and warm, perhaps freshly washed and moisturized.

I'm about to introduce myself, when she says, "I'm Qalixy. We've been expecting you," with an unrestrained smile. "Come this way."

I'm led down hallways that could serve as various definitions of crumbling, to a door simply marked "Lab C." Qalixy closes her eyes and seems to concentrate on some thought to unlock this door. Apparently it's equipped with a discreet mind scanner.

Inside "Lab C" the ceilings are also dilapidated, but the rest of the lab has a vintage modern atmosphere, not sleek and trendy but aesthetically unified by the recent design classics of curvaceous teak saddle-seat chairs, omni-directional orb lighting, silica filament shelving and cork flooring. We walk past obsidian countertops crammed with equipment, tools and electronic components, until we stop at one such countertop.

"Your friend's commission was quite a fascinating challenge," Qalixy says.

I don't bother to clarify what our relationship is; that doesn't seem important right now.

"The brief was one of our most... unusual, but the project was, in the end, well within our capabilities," she continues. "As you can see, the end product is quite... reasonable."

She places her hand on a small metal box we've been standing beside. Its glinting gray surfaces are featureless except for an on-off switch and dial on its top. This is apparently what I've been sent here for.

For a while, she doesn't say anything, perhaps letting me soak it in, appreciate the *reasonable* quality of this object. I wait for the explanation I have no hope of formulating from its nondescript form.

Then, when she thinks that I'm ready to know what it is, Qalixy tells me, "Its primary function is cardiotemporal resynchronization."

My eyes widen at this, as if to see the implications more clearly.

"Secondarily, it oscillates the psyche into a reason-receptive state," she adds.

"Does it perform both functions at the same time?" I ask.

"It can but doesn't have to. The details are in the instruction manual. But basically typical operation works like this: Have the subject hold the apparatus in their hands. Dial in the amount of force necessary. Then activate. It will pulse for a minute before automatically deactivating. If it seems like it wasn't effective, repeat those steps, with greater force if necessary."

I nod, imagining you holding this little metallic object as I flip the switch and step back to let it do its one minute of work on you.

"The next model will have an adjustable timer for the users to dial in the duration needed, but we've found that one minute is typically sufficient, and poses no danger of overshooting."

Qalixy is about to continue on with her explanation, but "overshooting" sounds like an important term.

So I ask, "What's that?"

"Ah, that's our term for exceeding the necessary amount of agitation from HJ2p."

Qalixy holds her right hand horizontal at chest level, then raises her left hand to over above it at head level, the space between them representing the excess perturbation.

"And what happens if there is overshooting?"

"For ethical reasons, it's difficult to test those scenarios, but over-energizing would typically result in restlessness, giddiness, confabulation, hyper-empathy, insomnia, wanderlust. Those kinds of things. But as the energy dissipates, the subject would eventually return to their healthy baseline."

She lowers her left hand to rest upon the back of her right one, which is still held at chest level.

"Oh," I murmur while telling myself to look for mentions of "overshooting" in the instructions.

"A requirement of the project brief was to make the final product portable, hence the size. We've also made a padded case for it."

Qalixy pulls open the drawer just beneath the countertop and removes a rust-orange leather pouch with a matching leather strap. It looks like it could be a vintage artisanal case for a compact, ornate set of binoculars. The stitching is impeccable.

With a few hours of daylight remaining, I make the return trip. Now and then, I glance at the leather pouch, as if to make sure it's real, like I'm transporting it out of a dream and into reality. It dangles by my waist, its strap hanging on my shoulder, diagonally crossing my torso like a thin sash officially marking my duty as courier between the realms of fantasy and ordinary.

A short ways past the Murlani River, I stop at a diner for a snack. As I have a bowl of garlic noodles with blanched vegetables, my eyes are drawn repeatedly to the mopey guy down the counter. Slumped over the bowl of macaroni and cheese, he looks like he's waiting for the epiphany that will inspire him to devour the pasta and proceed vigorously onward with his life. He could probably benefit from this device. But I don't want to risk him dropping it or some other mishap.

On the Resdwol Express, I doze off for a few minutes, then wake with a start. My hand closest to where it should be jerks to the little leather case. It's still there, full and solid with its contents. Soon, as the train reaches the city limits, the sun is setting.

When I get home, I am wiped out, and my clothes are thoroughly dusty. I should get some rest, but curiosity gets the better of me. After washing up and snacking on leftovers, I read the instruction manual. It describes the mechanism of action (pulsation of raw emotional energy) and diagrammatically shows the internal components with multi-word technical names like "dualistic inversional chronologous isotropilizer" and "retro-episodical etherealgial nullifier" and "deambiguational polyconstruance isolizer."

Once I've got a working understanding of what it'll do for you, I give in to exhaustion and curl up in bed.

The next morning, I wake up later than usual but just as refreshed as ever. I head over to your place. Traffic on the bike path is light, and as I hoped I would, I arrive in time to catch you before you head to work.

When you open the door to let me in, it takes me only a fraction of a second to know from your face that nothing has substantially changed. So before you can say anything, I tell you, "Here, hold this," and present you with the device you've commissioned.

As it rests on the palm of your right hand, your fingers curled upward around it, I flip the switch before you can ask any questions.

The thing whirs into operation. Your fingers tighten around it. I can't tell if that's to keep steady hold of the little box or because you want to more intensely feel the HJ2p's power, but you clutch it as if to make it part of you, to be bonded physically to the metallic object.

In the minute that follows, I watch your eyes brighten, your face beginning to glow just a little.

"Wow," you murmur once the box in your hand has stopped humming.

"So this is what they came up with?" you ask, your voice no longer sounding old beyond your years.

"Yes, this is it."

"Well, it was certainly worth it then. It worked!" you rejoice.

Relief enters me like sunlight shining right into the core of my being. The little box has snapped you right out of it.

"I really must run," you tell me, excitement pushing into the very edges of your voice. "I've got to get to the chronography lab to calibrate the synchronizers, but let's talk tonight. Come over for dinner?"

"You bet," I reply heartily, unable to be anything but ebullient now.

"Terrific! Do you want to have some juice or sit down while I finish getting ready?"

"No, that's all right, thanks. I'll see you tonight."

You nod, then kiss me on the cheek and smile as you vanish behind the closing door.

10 hours later, I'm back at your door. It feels like I'm somehow completing a particular symmetry to my day, your place and mine bookending my waking hours.

You let me in, all smiles and wide eyes. I take off my jacket and roll up my sleeves, to get to work in the kitchen. But on my way there, I see that you've got dinner all laid out on your compact square of a dining table.

When you see me staring at the zucchini casserole, you tell me, "I got to leave work early. I said it was a special occasion."

"And it is," I reply.

"Yes, I suppose it is," you agree with a smile.

I sit down in the chair by the patio door. You plate some casserole for us, then take the seat across from me.

"So how's work going?" you ask.

"Good, good. The exercises I'm doing with my clients are really paying off, and we're all growing tremendously. Except... "

Noticing that you're eating, I stop myself.

"Well, never mind," I decide aloud. "I don't want to end up venting my frustrations or something like that."

"No, don't you worry about that. What is it?"

"Well, tomorrow I've got a creativity coaching session with this client who *barely* follows up on the action items we've agreed upon at the end of each session. Today, I was supposed to get an update from him, so that I can better prepare for our meeting. I received nothing, so he's probably going to come in with very little progress and therefore very little for us to work off of."

I sigh heavily, then both of us are eating in silence. The casserole piques my palate with Gorgonzola and ample garlic flavors lightly coating the succulent, thick zucchini slices.

"That does sound frustrating," you remark.

"Yes. We need to discuss discipline, but I've been dreading that. So much so that I'm thinking of not making a big deal of it and just mentioning how important followup is—*again*. Hopefully the repetition will get the message across. The alternative is to have some straight talk about how he's disrespecting our time together, disrespecting his potential and the people in his life who support him. That'll probably be ugly but helpful. I don't know. Maybe I should get over my discomfort and just make it ugly."

"Yes, you should. Just use fear displacement to push yourself to have that talk," you say offhandedly.

I wait for you to elaborate, but you turn your attention to the Brussels sprouts and spoon some on to your plate.

"Fear displacement?" I prompt you as you reach a spoonful of Brussels sprouts over to my plate. They cascade down beside the remaining casserole, like little cabbages tumbling out of a dimension of dwarf vegetables.

"Surely you must have a fear about this situation that's greater than the fear of having an upsetting conversation with him," you reply. "Like the fear of not living up to your responsibilities as a coach, or later regretting that you weren't true to your values."

My eyes widen as you say this.

"What are you *more afraid of* that will put this fear in its place?" you ask.

"You're absolutely right. I can't believe I hadn't thought about that. I'm afraid of wasting time and missing opportunities. Afraid of looking back months from now and finding that we made little progress because we didn't tackle his discipline problem."

"That makes a lot of sense. In fact, you could tell him that, and even if he doesn't get his act together, he'll very clearly know why you want him to, why it's worth having a conversation that could upset both of you."

"Yeah, you're right. It all seems so obvious now," I marvel. "Thanks, that's a load off my mind!"

"No problem. It feels like you took a load off my heart this morning, so I'm happy to return the favor."

"I'll have to try fear displacement on other decisions and situations too," I decide.

You nod encouragingly and say, "It's great when you can use emotional exclusion positively and practically."

"Emotional exclusion?"

"You know, how it's difficult to fully experience more than one emotion at a time. It's hard for emotional states to coexist in the mind. When you're feeling a mixture of emotions, you're usually switching through different emotional states. It could be that one emotion is triggering another, which re-triggers the first emotion or another emotion entirely."

"Oh, wow, I can't believe I never noticed that."

"But it takes reflection to notice, which we're not immediately adept at and needs to be done more deliberately. Speaking of which, I'm thinking we should go to Moltani during the equinox. Really reflective atmosphere there. You'll wonder why the whole city isn't full of philosophers. Fabulous food and splendid weather during the equinox."

"But we're not even at the *solstice* yet," I exclaim.

"Right, so before you know it, the equinox will be just around the corner."

I can't argue with that, and what you go on to describe sounds absolutely enticing—you and I in abundant sunlight and gently warm air, sampling the intellectual delicacies of the area, picnicking in valleys speckled with wildflowers, nature's beautiful little mysteries all around us.

As I bicycle home, I'm warmed by a delightful exhaustion, the kind of wonderful fatigue that only comes after talking excitedly with you about life. But this mood is tinged with vague unease. You're back to normal now but in some peculiar way *more* than normal. You talk with such easygoing confidence in your perspectives. Maybe I'm just imagining things. Maybe it's been too long since I've seen you fully in the present. Only, it seems like you're not quite fully in the present in another way.

Maybe the problem lies with my expectations, with the comparisons I'm unconsciously making between your behavior now and how you've acted in the past. Maybe you can't go back to "normal," who you used to consistently be. Maybe this is the new normal for you.

Whatever it is, you're better than you've been recently, and for that I'm thankful.

Still excited by your dramatic turnaround, I ecstatically spend more time with you in the following weeks than I have in the past several months.

Over these weeks, the little incidents during our celebratory dinner grow into trends. You casually use terminology I've never heard of, sprinkling phrases like *possibility density* and *consistency sensitivity* into our conversations as if they're just common knowledge.

When I tell you that concerns about my clients are cutting disruptively into miscellaneous moments of my day, you reply succinctly with, "Sounds like you need to characterize, then actively steward the ecologies of your subjective time."

I nod, your words striking a chord in me, even though I have to guess at the specific meaning you're trying to convey.

The next day, I look up the phrase "ecology of subjective time" and variants of it in the community concept library. I get no useful results. You must have come up with this phrase or gleaned it from some obscure source.

When we're hanging out in the new waffle cafe and then when we're hiking, you describe intricate plans to establish a cognitive engineering institute; you tell me all about the teams the staff will be organized into, the kinds of projects they'll be working on, the breakthroughs in thought they might unlock, the way this work will quietly incite a revolution in human cognition to depose the tyranny of antiquated heuristics.

With this ever unfolding story, it's like you're fast-forwarding past whole chunks of your career.

"Even though it hits the sweet spot of affordability and economic vitality, Rolono Dervnal is just too low on the inspiration index to ever warrant serious consideration about relocating or even visiting there," you told me as we soaked in the local hot-spring bathhouse. "Spending time there is really only a viable option if you need a place that's cognitively under-stimulating, so you can just relax and put creativity and wonder on hold."

Inspiration index? I had no idea anyone quantified the extent to which a place is inspiring.

You develop a habit of avoiding badly designed objects, as if ranking things you use with that inspiration index—inspiration not in the epiphanal sense but the motivational sense—choosing to only have contact with objects that can fit into an elegantly streamlined workflow or thoughtfully curated life of beauty and productivity.

You get into the habit of habit curation, the tweaking of long-held habits you like, the adoption of new ones, the obliteration of old ones.

It's unmistakably an effort to build your future self's lifestyle now, to set up a pattern of daily structure this self can comfortably inhabit.

Are you turning into a cerebral poet composing verses in the medium of your life, or daydreaming out loud into reality with intellectual fervor?

On my next day off—that day I set aside in every week to have no client sessions—I prepare a daypack and make the trip to the design consultancy again.

Along the way, I try to enjoy the scenery of the autumn landscape, but our recent conversations with all their novel jargon crowd my mind. They abbreviate my trip, condensing and truncating portions of it. The gondola ride is merely a blur of canyon trees and an overheard conversation about mental sculptures. The hour-long walk past the apple orchards feels like it lasted only ten minutes. Before I know it, I'm there.

"Hi," I urgently greet the receptionist.

"Hello," she says.

"I need to talk with Qalixy," I tell her.

"Please have a seat. I'll page her now."

A couple of minutes later, Qalixy walks in with a concerned smile.

"Hello again," she says. "What brings you back here?"

"I think HJ2p has had some side effects," I answer, not sure if I should get into specifics right here and now.

She nods and takes me down the hallway to a door marked "Thursday" and opens it for me to enter. A few of her colleagues are in this room, and we sit in a corner alcove that puts us at an almost distraction-free distance from them.

"Now, tell me *everything*," she instructs. "Even if something seems unimportant, mention it. Err on the side of abundance, of high granularity."

I start recounting recent events and observations in chronological order, but soon, I'm narrating with a more thematic approach, grouping your behaviors into patterns: your ever elaborating, idiosyncratic phraseology, a growing disconcern for intricacies of your current job, the vehement forging of future plans that leapfrog the present and just take for granted it'll run its course.

"Interesting," she muses after I explain everything.

"I mean, this doesn't really pose a problem. There's no real issue to speak of. But it is unusual, and I'd like to make sure it's not going to become something more concerning."

Qalixy nods thoughtfully, then looks up, to gaze out the skylight, as if to beam her thoughts to a cloud above us.

"Yes, yes, there was some risk of that," she says, like she's summed up everything I've mentioned in her mind, consolidated it all down into one phenomenon, condensed it into one term that in her mind captures all the details.

"Risk of what?" I ask.

She looks at me and says, "Tell me," as if ignoring my question, but I sense she is building a prelude to its answer. "Would you describe your friend as a forward thinker? Someone whose thoughts are at the forefront of contemplations on modern life?"

"Yes, actually. Yes, I would say that's a good characterization."

"Okay, that probably explains it. You see, had we more time and resources, we would have assessed the effects of HJ2p and its successors on various personality types. To understand how different dispositions are specifically impacted. But, we do have preliminary test results suggesting that for forward thinkers, HJ prototypes and early production models could jostle their minds into the future, because they are already future leaning. Or at least their minds are jostled into further consideration of the future.

We're not really sure exactly what happens there, whether they are actually temporally dislocated or simply perceive themselves as being and therefore thinking in the future. Either way, from our point of view, it would be like they're ahead of our time. That's probably what's happened with your friend."

"Wow," I murmur.

"Don't worry. As with overshooting, this should self-rectify," Qalixy assures me. "Your friend should be back to baseline soon enough, once the extra energy has fully dissipated. But let us know if anything changes."

She places a hand firmly on my shoulder, as if I'm the one who is in the future, needing to be re-anchored to the present.

On my way home, Qalixy's explanation slowly creates ambivalence. I'm glad your situation isn't serious, and it's comforting to know that your thoughts will soon be more comprehensible to me. But *something* will be missing once the effects of HJ2p wear off. Then, as I'm wading through the Murlani River, trying not to become mesmerized by all the water undulating past me, it hits me in a flash of raw insight. But I can't really think about it until I've finished my crossing. The concentration on my footing crowds everything else out of my consciousness.

Seven minutes later, when I'm fully out of the water, sitting on the completely stationary riverbank, that insight rapidly organizes itself into prose. These days, you seem more you than you've ever been, now more actively and comfortably—*fervently* in the world of your thoughts. The fluidity with which you form and share your thoughts now rivals you at your most cogent in the past. You are at your most cognitively lucid now. Maybe you're meant to inhabit the future—that's where you're most at home.

So I decide that I'll help you more fully inhabit it now, at least mentally. As I leave the relentless flow of the Murlani behind, I start planning out what I'll mention in our next conversations.

How long does emotional residue last? When it's negative, should it be actively cleansed from relationships so that it doesn't tinge future interactions? Should the emotional lensing produced by residues be actively counteracted or somehow offset?

How long can thoughts hibernate in the unconscious mind before actively re-inhabiting the subjective timescape?

How do the places that appeal to you and the influences that you pay attention to rank in terms of the insight index?

"Oh my goodness, yes, the insight index," you'll say. "We'll need to plot that against the inspiration index to de-convolute these components of intellectual invigoration."

"Yes, and that could reveal to us how to reliably get into the sweet spots of the highly inspiring, highly insightful or situations and environments that are both," I'll say, extending your thoughts to their logical conclusion.

And you'll fervidly add, "Right, and *of course*, the intellectually affective space has high-order multidimensionality, but insight and inspiration form one of the most meaning-dense subspaces."

And then I'll realize why we get on so well together and why we're spending ever more time together now.

Untimely Resynchronization

As I'm taking a break with a mug of coffee in the rooftop garden, you show up, seemingly out of nowhere, as if just materializing in my little corner of the world, back into my life.

The cityscape all around us, your gaze grabs me by the heartstrings and holds my attention, commanding it without even trying. Like they're imbued with the very essence of the sky far above us, those intense yet relaxed violet eyes of yours reach right into my psyche. They resynchronize my heart to yours, bringing us both into the same cardiotemporal realm, placing us both in the same emotional moment. You're pulling me out of the time I've been inhabiting, removing me from the minutes and hours I've existed in. I enter a bubble that could last seconds or centuries, in which there is only you and me, our lives now set to the same rhythm.

With this, any possibility of completing project Zanslad is gone; all chances of it coming to fruition remain in the world that I've now lost contact with, no longer have agency in.

"Why do you have to show up now and pull me into this other now?" I manage to ask while in your thrall.

"Because life doesn't know any better than to throw two people disruptively, ecstatically together at inopportune times," you answer, the explanation unfurled so deftly that it must have been ready at your fingertips for insertion into conversations, like you've been asked this before and made the response part of your elevator pitch.

Your voice is warm and smooth, like glazed porcelain that's been out in the sun. I want to caress it all over.

I nod, this logic of life you've revealed ringing true in my mind, extending its explanatory power to pivotal events in my past.

"*Actually*," you say, "it's been a hobby of mine to keep tabs on you and plot out when I could most jostlingly re-enter your life."

"But why would you do that? Why derail me in such a drastic way? What have I done to you to warrant—*provoke* this?"

"Because by knocking you off course, that's when there's the best chance you'll find something greater, something we can discover together. The stakes have to be high."

I believe you—I have no choice but to believe you as our minds settle into their cognitive symbiosis, yours setting the tone, determining the landscape all around us, the one we must now venture into.

As the Arsenal Expands

Across the wooden picnic table she slides towards me a smile. Simply and mysteriously a smile. Clearly, it's not her own.

In fact, I don't recognize it at all. If I had seen it before, I'd definitely remember the natural charm fully in its possession.

For a while, I just look at it. At the taut, joyful curvature lying before me.

Then, finally, I look at her. Her face is utterly stolid, like the giddiness of yesterday afternoon had never existed, is now negated from the past by her composure.

Thinking—*hoping*—maybe she's borrowed it from someone, maybe even from someone slightly famous, I ask her, "Whose is it?"

"No one's. Yet," she answers.

"You've begun a career in smile forging?" I try.

"No, though maybe I should. That would be lucrative."

Then we're quiet, me looking at the smile again, she looking at me. A warm gust of wind rustles the lush summertime foliage of the aspens and beeches around us, this jostling of leaves like the echo of a downpour from a parallel universe.

"So are you going to tell me what this is about?" I ask.

"No more guesses?"

"You found it?"

"Oh, *man*, if only it were that easy."

"Well, that's all I've got, a guess that's not even logically consistent with what you said earlier."

"Okay, I'll show you. Put it in your pocket."

I recoil at this imperative.

"I don't want *that* in my pants," I blurt.

"Oh, *grow up*," she says. "This isn't some twisted joke or surreal gag."

"All right," I concede, picking up the attractive curvature of lips.

It is both calm and exuberant on my fingertips. I place it in my right pocket, completely away from the keys in my left one.

"Great," she says, then places a temper bottle on the middle plank of the table.

Through its translucent body, I see the contents seething.

Before I can say anything, she gives it a shake, then twists the top of the bottle clockwise to set the release timer to omnidirectional dispersal in 30 seconds.

"Are you crazy?" I shout.

I grab for the bottle to reset its containment parameters before the agitated contents explode everywhere and spew raw anger all over us. But before my hands can get anywhere near it, she snatches the bottle away from me.

"Use the smile," she says, voice taut and austere.

Too scared to do anything else, I do as she has bade me, quickly removing the smile from my pocket and placing it on the table. Instantly, the timer on the bottle reverts to its default holding settings.

"Now you see?" she prompts more than asks.

"A disarming smile," I murmur, eyes still bulging.

"And it's going to be yours."

"What? *No*, I'm not going to wear that into dangerous situations."

"It's reliable, I assure you. And I *need you* to do me a favor. To chill out some volatile negotiations."

I just stare at her.

"You'll just seem to be there incidentally," she continues. "Merely passing through the lobby of the conference center. You'll flash the smile, and they'll all ease up."

"Won't they know? Someone flashes a smile, and suddenly the mood is all mellow—how can that not be suspicious?"

"Yes, it would be suspicious *if* they thought it were possible for a smile to change the atmosphere so fundamentally. You know how hard it is to make one of these? Getting the nonlocal multidimensional tunings right, that's like cooking dinner for your childhood role models with only three ingredients, one of which *isn't* saffron."

"I can imagine."

"Yes, I knew you'd appreciate the effort involved," she says, surely referring to my stints as a mood engineer.

I think this over. She would only make this request if the matter were truly important. And I do owe her for the construction of several existential anchoring objects, the clutching of which kept me stabilized when the implausibility storm hit at the end of winter. Doing this favor for her will probably make us even, but she's not pressuring me with that. Yet.

"All right," I agree.

She nods with quiet satisfaction.

"But I need to test this out. Make sure it's the real deal," I stipulate.

"Okay, take it for a spin," she encourages.

So I do.

And that's how I meet you.

Acknowledgements

I am deeply appreciative of...

Jenny, for tremendous, unwavering emotional support
Brian, for the Nespresso machine and desk that catalyzed much of this work
Sione, for all the thoughtful feedback
Melissa, for on-point pointers
Mara, for a uniquely encouraging and cerebral collaboration
Charlie, for the generosity of time and perspective
Black Lawrence Press, for *Sapling*—a steady stream of publishing possibilities (i.e. nuggets of hope)
Niall, for such thoughtful attention to the design and layout of this book

Thank you for making this story collection possible!

Soramimi Hanarejima is an informatics consultant who is ever curious about the structure of ideas and thought. Convinced that fiction can play an important role in exploring and developing metacognition, Soramimi writes stories to engage in literary experiments about thinking, in hopes of finding unique narrative insights.